THIS IS NOT A GAME

Lord Garquin and Lord Cain are no more. The civilization I created reduced to ashes. But that world was easy compared to what's up next. I have no control over Aqua Gen . . . or its inhabitants. The last time the AquaGens were visited by an alien race, things didn't go so well.

The Alpha team needs you. Solve the codes in this book at VoyagersHQ.com and help us avoid the pirates of Aqua Gen. The fate of Earth hangs in the balance. And we have no idea what the Omega team is planning. . . .

Chris,
Ship Specialist I Alpha Team

The AquaGens have lived in peace
for thousands of years.
Until now . . .

OMEGA RISING

VOYAGERS

Don't miss a single Voyage. . . .

OMEGA RISING

Patrick Carman

Random House 🏠 New York

Text copyright © 2016 by PC Studios Inc.
Full-color interior art, puzzles, and codes copyright © Animal Repair Shop
Voyagers digital and gaming experience by Animal Repair Shop

All rights reserved. Published in the United States by Random House
Children's Books, a division of Penguin Random House LLC, New York.

Random House and the colophon are registered trademarks of
Penguin Random House LLC.

Visit us on the Web! randomhousekids.com

Educators and librarians, for a variety of teaching tools,
visit us at RHTeachersLibrarians.com

VoyagersHQ.com

Library of Congress Cataloging-in-Publication Data
is available upon request.
ISBN 978-0-385-38664-7 (trade) — ISBN 978-0-385-38666-1 (lib. bdg.) —
ISBN 978-0-385-38665-4 (ebook)

Printed in the United States of America
10 9 8 7 6 5 4 3 2 1
First Edition

For Michelle Nagler, Mallory Loehr, John Adamo,
Mary McCue, John Sazaklis, Lisa Nadel, Jenna Lettice,
Caroline Abbey, Barbara Marcus, and the whole Voyagers
team at Penguin Random House—without whom the world
of Voyagers would not exist. Thank you for fighting so hard
and always staying positive. You are my Team Alpha!
—P.C.

Ship's log 12.12

[Alpha team member: Dash Conroy]

[Comm link: audio feed, *Cloud Cat*]

This is Dash Conroy, leader of the Voyagers Alpha team. Everything that could have gone wrong did go wrong. We're lucky to be alive.

[A seven-second break in the message occurs here.]

We are currently missing one member of our team. The situation on the surface is too unstable for reentry. I'm on the deck of the Cloud Cat, *staring down at a tornado churning the watery surface of Aqua Gen.*

[A four-second break in the message occurs here.]

If I can't bring our teammate back, I will resign my post effective immediately.

[End of transmission]

26 Hours Earlier.

The flight deck of the *Cloud Leopard* was buzzing with ZRKs as Carly Diamond moved closer to the curved forward window. They'd only been out of Gamma Speed for a few hours, and the ZRKs were busy testing every system on the ship for possible damages. Carly stared down at the liquid surface of a planet, shimmering in the light of a sun not her own.

"Now that's what I call an ocean," she said, shaking her head with amazement. "It's a planet-sized water ball."

Gabriel Parker and Piper Williams came up beside her.

"I knew I should have packed my fishing gear," Gabriel said. "I'd love to hook into whatever's lurking around down there."

Piper glanced back and forth at the sides of her air chair and felt it wobble slightly, reacting to her movements. "I can't swim," she observed. "Unless this contraption has a setting I don't know about."

Dash was checking his MTB—Mobile Tech Band—where a message from Chris had just arrived: *Planetary briefing on the main bridge in two minutes. I'll be right there.*

Dash looked up and locked eyes with Piper. He knew he had to handle the situation delicately.

"Aqua Gen is completely covered in water. And it's deep," Dash said. "Deeper than our deepest oceans on

Earth." He shook his head for effect. "The extraction team will almost certainly have to be in the water at some point."

Piper's eyes narrowed, and her jaw tightened. He knew that look of determination. "Not that you couldn't handle it," Dash rushed to say. "But there's no sense putting anyone at unnecessary risk if we don't have to."

This seemed to resonate with Piper. A little.

STEAM 6000 made a few beeping sounds, like his electronic brains were calculating a big problem, and he started reeling off statistics in his tinny voice.

"Combined scoring in the submarine and watercraft training resulted in the following data: Gabriel—mission-ready. Carly—mission-ready. Dash—ninety-one percent mission-ready. Piper—"

"Don't say it," Piper interrupted. She moved her air chair a few feet over everyone's heads and flew in an aggressive circle. Sometimes it was how she cooled off.

"She can really fly that thing," Carly said.

"Impressive, yes sir!" STEAM 6000 said. "Piper— sixty-seven percent mission-ready."

Dash shook his head and stared at the floor. "STEAM, you're killing me here."

Piper hovered within an inch of STEAM's head and glared at him. "I could do it if I had to. The water just freaks me out, is all. I can't help feeling like I'm going to drown."

"Totally understandable," Dash offered.

"We got this one," Gabriel added. He cracked his knuckles for good measure. "I am so ready to ride those watercraft. Let's do this!"

Dash was equally concerned and excited by Gabriel's self-assurance. He could always count on Gabriel to throw himself into challenges with everything he had. But Gabriel was a big risk taker. And with a small crew literally light-years from Earth, risk was something Dash could only accept in small doses.

Chris arrived on deck, holding a tablet in one hand. He tapped out a few commands and set the tablet down on the floor. A hologram of a watery planet appeared in the middle of the group. "Aqua Gen. It's like nothing we've seen so far. It will be dangerous."

"I like what I'm hearing," Gabriel said. "The whole planet is poisonous water, right? No, wait—the Loch Ness monster is down there, only he's bigger than Godzilla. He's like a building with claws and teeth!"

"Gabriel, please," Dash said.

"Sorry," Gabriel said, but he couldn't help himself. "You know what a water planet has to have? Pirates! No, wait, *zombie* pirates!"

Carly punched Gabriel in the shoulder. "Zombie pirates," she echoed, rolling her eyes.

Dash smiled. "Carly, stop hitting the other crew members."

Chris put a hand out and spun the holographic globe, a grave look on his face: "Gabriel, you're more right than you know."

Piper drifted in closer. STEAM whirled to life and rolled closer too. Gabriel leaned in.

"I gotta know," Gabriel said. "Is it pirates or monsters or both?"

And with that, Chris began the briefing for a perilous journey into the sea of Aqua Gen.

"**Okay, so that's** more messed up than I was expecting," Gabriel said.

Chris had finished most of the briefing when he was interrupted by a beep from his MTB. He checked the message, then picked up the tablet. The hologram of Aqua Gen vanished. "A team of ZRKs is having trouble with the *Cloud Cat* landing gear repair. I'll see to it while you discuss the rest of the plan."

With a nod, Chris handed the tablet to Dash and headed for the *Cloud Cat.*

"Are these Thermites really twenty feet long?" Carly asked.

"The fully grown ones are, yeah," Dash confirmed, scrolling through planetary data on the screen.

"And they're like a snake, only they've got suction cups like an octopus and inside those are tons of little teeth?" Piper asked.

"That's correct," Dash said matter-of-factly. He tapped the tablet screen a few more times, searching for information. "There are approximately six million of them down there, give or take. But they're slow and easy to track. They travel in schools of several thousand, so we can spot them from far away. Shouldn't be a problem."

"It sounds like a problem to me," Carly said.

Dash was determined to downplay the dangers they would encounter on Aqua Gen, because the reality was far too frightening. He kept his voice calm and assured.

"Moving on to Predator Z," Dash said. "They travel alone, so that's good. Data confirms they look and act like a giant prehistoric alligator. A fully grown Predator Z runs about sixty feet. They're kind of fast. And hungry. These we really need to avoid."

"How many are down there?" Gabriel asked.

STEAM made a few beeping sounds. "More than eight thousand, less than one million."

Gabriel rolled his eyes. "Not helpful."

"You guys, this is all going to be fine. It's a get-in, get-out operation," Dash said. "Aqua Gen is a big planet. The chances of us encountering anything that's alive are slim."

STEAM started to beep some more, and Dash stared bullets at the robot. Dash didn't need statistics on possible encounters with indigenous sea creatures that could kill them. It would be much tougher if they went into the mission afraid of never coming back. "STEAM, could you do me a favor and go find Chris? He needs to get back here for this."

The robot started to speak, but Dash cut him off. "Now would be good. Thanks, buddy."

STEAM made a sad sort of turn and moved slowly

across the flight deck of the ship, but he called back before he was at the door.

"Forty-seven percent chance of encounter with Predator Z, sixty percent chance of encounter with Thermites."

STEAM went into double-speed mode and left the deck.

"He just couldn't keep his big robot mouth shut, could he?" Carly muttered.

"Look, you guys, we're going to be okay. You heard Chris—the landing site is secure and we have amazing equipment. We've taken down a Raptogon; we've survived a robot war and a molten river of fire. There's nothing this planet can throw at us that we can't handle. We're Voyagers. We got this."

Everyone looked down nervously at the blue-and-green water of Aqua Gen.

"What else?" Carly asked. "And don't tell me there are zombie pirates down there."

Dash looked sheepishly at the ceiling and then his crew.

"No zombies. But, umm, there *are* pirates."

"No way!" Piper said. "You are totally making that up."

"I wish I was," Dash conceded, and just when he felt like he needed backup, Chris returned to the deck.

Chris strode into the room confidently. Five ZRKs hovered around him like bees near a hive as he quickly relayed a series of commands. A moment later, the ZRKs were gone, headed back to the *Cloud Cat* for final repairs. Rocket trotted happily behind Chris until he saw the Alpha team and ran over. Rocket was Chris's golden retriever, and everyone saw him as the ship's mascot. He was the friendliest dog in the known universe.

"I just got to the part about the pirates," Dash said.

"Ah yes, those," Chris said. There was a smidge of concern in his voice, which was a lot for Chris.

Chris took several long strides across the deck and looked down at the planet with the rest of them. "The AquaGens have been visited before," he said, worriedly staring at the surface of the planet. "It did not go well."

"What does that mean?" Gabriel asked.

Chris seemed to be calculating his answer, like a champion chess player assessing the board.

"The AquaGens are fierce when they need to be," he said slowly. "But they are a peaceful people at heart. They are intelligent beings with a developed language you'll be able to translate with our advanced technology."

"And these pirates," Carly said. "What about them?"

"While I was visiting Aqua Gen, someone else invaded this planet. These alien visitors became sort of like pirates of the planet, and have wreaked havoc ever since. They have destabilized the order of the AquaGens."

"What a bunch of jerks. Who takes over someone else's planet?" Carly asked, her eyes narrowing.

Chris looked once more at the watery surface. "They are illusive and dangerous, these pirates. But we don't know much else about them."

"Bummer," Gabriel said. "But they're not zombies, right?"

"No, Gabriel. They are not zombies," Chris admitted as he moved toward the middle of the flight deck. Rocket followed obediently, wagging his tail. When Chris turned back, there was a grave look on his face. "It will be best if you're not seen by anyone."

"Got it," Dash said. "The AquaGens are already leery of visitors from the outside world, so we need to stay clear of everyone on this planet if we can."

Chris looked down at Rocket and made a motion with his hand that had an alien quality to it. Rocket walked over to Piper's air chair and sat down, staring up happily.

STEAM returned and pulled up next to Chris. "The ZRKs are reporting trouble with the slogger."

Chris's attention turned entirely to the robot. "What's the status?"

STEAM made a few whirling sounds and then answered: "Code red dash nine."

For the second time in a matter of minutes, a concerned look crossed Chris's face.

"The ship and the mission are yours," Chris said, looking gravely at Dash. "Proceed with caution."

And then Chris strode quickly off the deck.

Dash gazed one last time at the blue-green surface of Aqua Gen.

"Looks like we might be on our own this time."

2

"**The element we** picked up on Meta Prime is unstable," Dash explained. "If it leaks out of our little slogger buddy, that element will eat right through the hull of our ship. Magnus 7 is an element that should be carefully monitored."

"Poor TULIP," Piper said. "She has a big job."

"Why couldn't we have picked a slogger with a tougher name?" Gabriel asked. "I'd be more comfortable knowing the hottest substance in the universe was being held in place by Vlad the Magnus 7 Impaler."

The Alphas all laughed. It was good to feel a little relief.

"Hey, I like TULIP's name," Carly said after a minute. "I'll defend that tough little slogger's honor if no one else will! She won't fail us."

"It's nothing Chris can't handle," Dash said confidently. "He built the *Cloud Leopard*. I think he can work through some slogger modifications."

"Let the genius alien do his work," Gabriel said

confidently. "We can handle getting the—what was it called again?"

"Pollen Slither," Carly said.

"Maybe if you say it real slow he'll remember this time," Piper joked. "Pollllliiiiiiiiin Slitherrrrrr."

"Loopy Slather?" Gabriel asked. He wasn't going to let Piper have the last joke.

"I'm glad everyone is feeling relaxed," Dash said, and he meant it. "Let's show Chris we can make this extraction smooth. We get in, we get out, we hightail it to the next planet."

"I like the way you lead, leader person," Gabriel said.

Dash gave each team member a list of prelaunch tasks and sent them scattering in different directions. They would depart in under an hour, and he had something to complete before they all met at the *Cloud Cat* docking bay.

Dash stopped in front of the first tube opening he came to and tapped out a few instructions on a control pad next to it. The tubes were one of his favorite parts of the ship. On the *Cloud Leopard*, the crew members didn't get from place to place by walking stairs or taking elevators. They used a complicated system of tubes that ran through the guts of the ship in a thousand different ways.

"Gabriel, how'd you do that?" Dash asked.

The leaderboard on the display pad showed that Gabriel had logged the longest route yet only hours ago. He hadn't mentioned it. Gabriel wanted Dash to find it on his own.

Dash took a long look at the route map and slid his finger along a series of dots that would determine his path, taking him from point A to point B but in the longest, twistiest way he could. Then he grabbed the bar above the hole with both hands and threw his feet in like he was entering a waterslide. The wild ride took him back and forth around sharp curves on a pocket of air in a twisting, falling, rising pathway.

The vast engine room loomed up in front of Dash as he reached his destination. He looked back at the tube and saw he had not beaten Gabriel's or even Carly's longest route. The control pad showed him still several feet of tubing behind them both. Dash was tempted to try again, but thought better of it.

"Chris? You in here?" Dash yelled.

Steam poured off pipes and colossal metal structures, all part of an engine that could achieve something far faster than the speed of light. ZRKs were everywhere, replacing small rivets and changing out parts. Chris didn't answer, but Dash saw him at the far end of the engine room.

Dash looked at his MTB, a device that resembled the top half of a tube sock. The crew all pulled it onto their arms every morning. Dash was cutting it close for his next shot, something he couldn't miss without potentially dire consequences. This was a secret only he and Chris knew about, and Dash was glad he had at least one person to lean on when it came to the topic of living or dying. Dash had started the Voyagers mission knowing he was six months too old. Gamma Speed would soon wreak havoc on his metabolism, and the daily injections were designed by Chris to keep him alive.

"Hey, Chris," Dash said. "I need my shot like five minutes ago. Do you have the kit with you?"

Chris put up a hand and silenced Dash. Even the ZRKs responded to Chris's motion for quiet, all of them stopping what they were doing at once. Chris was leaning into TULIP, the small robot slogger from Meta Prime, listening like a safecracker. Suddenly, he picked up a ball-peen hammer and slammed it against the side of TULIP's hull. TULIP made an *ACK GACK GARK* noise and shook back and forth for about three seconds. Then she was silent.

Chris set the hammer down and turned to Dash as all the ZRKs went buzzing back to work.

"Looks like real precision work you're doing there," Dash said.

"It's more delicate than it appears," Chris said.

Dash found that hard to believe, but then, Chris had invented the sloggers. Chances were he knew what he was doing.

"So about that shot?" Dash asked.

Chris picked up a small kit and took out an instrument that looked like a futuristic thermometer.

Dash cocked his head. "Dude, I am not putting that weird thing in my mouth."

Before Dash could say another word, the thermometer was halfway up his nose.

"Don't move," Chris said stoically. "It's quite close to your brain cavity. Just another second and we're all done."

Dash froze, imagining the strange metal object next to the smooshiness of his brain. When Chris yanked it out, Dash felt a zing in his head like he'd licked an electric fence.

"What was that?" Dash yelled. "It felt like you stuffed a Taser up my nose!"

Chris didn't say anything as he stared at the device. He picked up the ball-peen hammer with his free hand and thwacked TULIP again. TULIP made a loud *FWEEEEEEE* sound and appeared to sneeze.

"Your vitals are holding just fine," Chris reported. "But the rate we're traveling puts us approximately seven-point-six days behind schedule. We need to get back into Gamma Speed as quickly as we can."

Dash rubbed the side of his nose. As Chris prepared the daily dose of the biologic that was designed to keep Dash alive in space, Dash seriously wondered if he could make up more than a week of lost time.

Dash administered the injection himself as Chris prepared to go back to work on TULIP.

"Unless absolutely necessary, do not interrupt me. This phase of work on TULIP requires a seamless attention to detail. It's going to take quite a bit of time."

"We can handle Aqua Gen," Dash said with more assurance than he was really feeling. If an alien of Chris's intelligence needed that much space to do the work, it must be seriously complex—or dangerous. Dash didn't really want to think too much about it.

"Don't underestimate what Piper can bring to this mission," Chris said as he turned away, picked up the hammer, and stared at the slogger. "She may yet turn out to be more valuable on Aqua Gen than you think."

"Will do," Dash agreed as he started for the *Cloud Cat* docking bay. He didn't get very far before an audio message came in on his MTB.

"Dash? It's Piper. We're at the docking station, but there's no sign of Carly. She's not answering my calls. Do you want me to go looking for her?"

Dash paused before answering. Carly was a reliable second-in-command. If she was late, she would have a good reason to be.

"Stay with the *Cloud Cat,* I'll find her," Dash said.

As Dash made a long tube ride through the inner workings of the ship, Carly sat alone in her room strumming the guitar she'd brought with her on the voyage. She played a soft, sad song her mother had taught her. She was thinking about leaving the *Cloud Leopard* for the first time and what she might encounter on an alien planet so many millions of miles from home.

"Sounds nice."

Carly jumped at the sound of Dash's voice. "Don't sneak up on me like that! You scared me half to death."

"Sorry," Dash said. "I didn't mean to startle you."

She knew she'd overreacted, but her nerves were on edge. Carly went back to playing and tried to ignore Dash. There was comfort in playing music. She could escape into it and forget about all the dangerous things outside her room. Her fingers flew across the strings as she sensed Dash moving a little closer.

"If I had a hundred years, I could never learn to play like that," Dash said. "It's a real gift."

Carly still didn't stop, and as Dash got close enough to see her face, he could tell that she was really upset.

"Hey, you okay?" he asked.

Her hand strummed the strings one last time, and Carly let the guitar rest in her lap. "My sister is better. And she's two years younger."

"Sounds like a competitive family," Dash said. "I never had to deal with that."

Carly tried to smile; she didn't want Dash seeing what she feared to be true: that somewhere up here in the middle of nowhere, galaxy unknown, she'd maybe lost something. Like her confidence.

"Do you miss them, your mom and your sister?" Carly asked. "Do you miss home?"

Dash took a deep breath. "I do. Always."

Carly looked up. "This is harder than I thought it was going to be."

Carly was pretty sure Dash would understand if she just told him the truth about how she felt, but what if she was wrong? What if he thought she was weak? It took her a few seconds, but finally she looked Dash in the eyes and continued.

"I'm afraid we're not going to make it back home. Actually, I'm just plain afraid. Aqua Gen sounds crazy, Dash."

Carly thought she saw a flash of concern move across Dash's face, but she couldn't be sure. Did Dash have the power to demote her to head guitar player or something like that? She was scared, but she still wanted to contribute. To do something important.

"I feel exactly the same way you do," Dash said, and Carly felt her spirits begin to lift. "We all do. But you're part of a team, a *family,* and we're going to get this done. And after that, I really do believe we're all going home."

Carly wasn't sure Dash felt the way he said he did about everything. But a leader had to be someone people would follow, and no one was going to follow Dash Conroy if he couldn't even make *himself* believe. She had to give him credit for trying.

"Okay," Carly said as she stood up and set the guitar aside. "Point taken. We've done things as hard as this before. And just as dangerous."

"And you've always been an important part of our success. You can do it again. I'm sure of it. Aqua Gen is going to be okay. You'll have your teammates to lean on.

We won't let you down, and we know you won't let us down either."

Carly nodded slowly.

"Can I meet you on deck?" she asked. "I just need a minute."

Dash nodded and moved for the door.

"And, hey, Dash?" Carly said.

"Yeah?"

"Gabe's right. You're pretty good at this leader stuff."

Dash smiled as he left the room, and Carly reached under her bed to pull out a small box. Inside were pictures of her family, which she kept for times like these. She couldn't always look at them or it made her too homesick, but sometimes she needed them.

"I'm coming home," she said confidently as she riffled through the pictures. "Count on it."

As Carly gathered herself for her very first trip to an alien planet, her mind shifted to being excited. She was going somewhere no human had ever gone before, and she was going there with her friends.

Meanwhile, Dash walked toward the main deck alone. His thoughts were anything but confident. His second-in-command was having a crisis of faith, and they were about to deploy on a planet full of pirates and sea monsters. Chris was basically off the grid. An alarming thermometer had been used to test his vitals, and he thought maybe his brain was leaking out of his nose.

Suddenly, the lights on the ship blinked off, and Dash was in utter darkness. Just as quickly, though, they came back up, flickering twice. *That was weird,* he thought. *System glitch?*

One thing was clear: the mission to Aqua Gen was not off to a good start.

Small beeps and whirls could be heard from inside a massive structure of computers and machines, but other than that, the room was quiet. Ike Phillips tapped out a few codes on a screen.

"This is Command, I need Anna Turner," he said.

A static-filled pause followed, and then Colin's voice shot back.

"It's good to hear your voice, Commander. What do you need?"

"I just said what I need. Anna Turner. Everyone else, leave us."

"I assure you, I can—" Colin said. His voice, like everything else about him, was an exact replica of Chris.

"I have my finger hovering over a console here," Ike said. "It's a kill switch. Do you know what that is, Colin?"

"Yes sir. I'll get Anna. Right away."

Colin looked across the bridge of the *Light Blade* with a wary eye. He was well aware of the kill switch, or at least the *idea* of the kill switch that Ike had theoretically planted in his head. Even across the galaxy, it was a switch that could supposedly put an end to Colin.

"Everyone but Anna, out," Colin said. Ravi, Niko, and Siena couldn't believe their ears. They were all gathered for the Aqua Gen briefing. Even SUMI, their onboard training robot, was there.

Colin was the angriest among them, but he didn't let it show. Ike had put him in charge of every mission so far. Why this sudden change? Didn't Ike know that Colin was the only real leader of the *Light Blade*? He begrudgingly left with the others.

Anna remained, a smug look on her face as everyone else marched off the main deck.

"The bridge is clear, sir. What can I do for you?"

Ike only stared blankly, and Anna wondered if the audio feed had been compromised. She was about to ask again when Ike spoke.

"You're the only one I completely trust, Anna. The only one who understands how important it is that we retrieve all the elements before the Alpha team does."

Anna loved having the keys to the kingdom.

"I love my son, but he's been tricked by this Chris character," Ike went on. His tone turned gloomy at the mention of Shawn Phillips. "It can't be helped. Shawn was always a dreamer. It will be his undoing."

"I understand" was all Anna could think to say.

"This power source we're racing to find, it will change the world forever. Whole nations will be reordered. It's imperative the Source end up in the right hands."

Anna felt a wave of satisfaction that she was on the right side of things.

"We need some insurance," Ike said, coming to the point. "A way to make sure the Alpha team won't try to lose us in space. Do you understand?"

Anna thought she did. She had always hated having to follow the Alpha team, but there had never been anything she could do about it. They had the coordinates for all the stops, she didn't. Still, Anna had little worry about being left in the cold outer limits of the universe. "Dash would never—"

Anna could see she was about to disappoint her commander before she finished, and changed course. "I get it, sir. What were you thinking?"

As Ike explained what needed to happen on Aqua Gen in order to assure their success, Anna listened to every detail.

"It's very important that you get this right," Ike said once he'd finished. "Can I count on you?"

"I can handle it," Anna said. "Consider it done."

"Very good! I knew you were the right person for the job."

Ike Phillips closed out the feed and looked about the room, satisfied. As a final act of treachery, he flipped the kill switch. Nothing happened to Colin, of course. The kill switch was a lie Colin had come to believe over many years. How else was he going to keep a cloned alien on a leash this far from home? It was one of many symbols of Ike's authority. It was a command he felt would grow by leaps and bounds very soon. Supremacy of the known world was within his grasp.

"Time to show my son what real power is."

As his crew drifted back into the command center, Ike Phillips plotted his complete takeover of the Voyagers mission.

Anna wasn't the only one who noted Ike's every word. Someone else was listening too: Colin. He had done some communication rewiring in the *Light Blade* that allowed him to listen in on conversations throughout the ship. He smiled at the thought of how it was he who was really in control. How Anna and Ike had a lot to learn about what Colin was capable of.

One thing was for sure.

His day would come.

Something about seeing Piper in the docking bay as the *Cloud Cat* prepared to lift off made Dash wonder if he'd made the right choice leaving her behind. Test scores didn't always determine the best person for the job—he'd learned that from personal experience. What had Chris said? *Don't underestimate what Piper can bring to this mission.*

"How would you guys feel about bringing Piper with us in the *Cloud Cat*?" Dash asked Carly and Gabriel. "To have her closer to the surface if something comes up."

"I thought we were going for an in-and-out extraction, nothing complicated?" Carly reminded him.

"Yeah, totally. We are. But Chris and STEAM are already on the main ship. We've got them to navigate if we need to move the *Cloud Leopard*. Nothing's going to happen there. Why not bring her along, you know, just in case?"

Carly and Gabriel smirked at each other.

"What?" Dash asked.

"We knew this wasn't going to be as easy as you were hoping," Gabriel said. "Never is."

Dash shrugged. "If there's one thing I'm learning out here, it's that things are always more complicated in real life than they are on a tablet."

"Especially in outer space," Carly added.

"Sure, bring Piper along for the ride," Gabriel said. "Can't hurt."

Dash felt his shoulders relax, as if everything just got lighter.

"Hey, Piper!" he said into his MTB.

Piper clicked on her comm. Rocket was barking excitedly, doing his canine best to wish them well.

"Chris and STEAM can manage things here," Dash said. "We need you with us."

Piper hesitated. It was a water planet, and there was

nothing she could do to suddenly become a swimmer. No amount of wishing was going to change that, even if things got out of control.

"You'll stay in the *Cloud Cat*," Dash said, reading her silence. "I just think you should be close by, in case we need something. We'll position you right outside the atmosphere, where the AquaGens can't see you. STEAM could pick us up remotely, but you've gotten so good at backup navigation. Better if we have a real person on deck."

In space—real outer space—Piper had fallen in love with navigation training almost as much as medicine. STEAM had put her through her paces on the long journey, and she'd mastered the *Cloud Cat* controls. She would never have the natural skills Gabriel had—he was off the charts—but she had to admit Dash was right.

Piper's apprehension seemed to fade away, and she drifted her air chair up the length of the ramp into the *Cloud Cat* with Rocket close behind.

"Welcome aboard, Piper," Dash said. "And, uh, Rocket." Dash, Carly, Gabriel, and Piper exchanged a look, then laughed.

"It looks like this will be Rocket's first voyage to a distant planet too," Carly said with a smile.

Rocket wagged his shaggy tail and barked.

"Ready to get this show on the road?" Gabriel asked.

"Ready," Carly and Dash said at the same time. Carly shook off what little nervousness remained, while Dash looked at his team, feeling good about every one of them.

"Ready," Piper echoed.

"Bring us in at zero mark fifty," Dash said. Gabriel already plotted out their options and found a location entirely empty of life. No one on Aqua Gen was ever going to know they'd been visited by Voyagers.

"Zero mark fifty," Gabriel said, pushing the *Cloud Cat* into high gear as it blasted away from the docking bay. The smaller ship, about the size of an average house, wobbled under the power of its thrusters.

"Take it easy, Gabriel," Dash said. "Remember what Chris said: low profile."

But as usual, Gabriel was unable or unwilling to tone down his use of the Voyagers equipment. He was like a NASCAR driver; if Gabriel was behind the wheel of a race car with a track in front of him, there was only one choice: gun it.

"I'm bringing us in about twenty feet from the surface," Gabriel reported. "We'll deploy the watercraft from there."

"I tested all the watercraft instruments in the pre-mission phase," Carly said. "Best I can tell everything checked out okay."

"It's a good thing we can't locate the element from up here," Gabriel said. "Otherwise we wouldn't have a chance to take those babies out for a spin."

The crew stopped talking as the ship accelerated. Dash gripped his armrests as his back pushed firmly into his seat. They were coming in hotter than Dash liked, nose down toward the watery surface of Aqua Gen.

"Pull back, Gabriel. You're heading in too steep."

"Oh, ye of little faith," Gabriel said as he expertly tilted the front of the *Cloud Cat.* They hovered precisely twenty feet above the surface of the water.

The pressure the crew felt instantly subsided as the ship leveled and slowed. Rocket, who had been sitting on Carly's lap, barked once with what Carly felt sure was appreciation.

"Piper, take the helm," Dash said.

Piper moved her air chair to a predetermined location at the front of the *Cloud Cat.* After she'd cleared level 9 navigation training, STEAM and a team of ZRKs had retrofitted a locking hub for Piper to dock her chair. She settled in, and Rocket leapt from Carly's lap to sit obediently at Piper's side.

"I have the controls," Piper said, and she couldn't help smiling as she stared out at the serene surface of Aqua Gen.

The rest of the crew moved off the main deck and into the cargo hold at the rear. There Dash saw three personal watercraft and one submarine. The submarine was shaped like a twelve-foot torpedo, with two seats and controls that were dug into the center, like a kayak. It was a two-person vehicle, but the element extraction controls were only in front of one seat. Dash planned to complete the extraction himself because it was more dangerous than he'd let on. There was nothing safe about finding yourself twenty thousand feet under the surface of an endless sea. But the sub would have to wait; it was the watercraft they needed now.

The watercraft were shaped like a wishbone, with a single seat positioned in the center of the Y. Propulsion came from the twin jet engines at the tail ends of the Y, and all the mapping tools were in the long front nose. They were sleek, beautiful machines, cast in blue-and-green camouflage to match the surface.

"Man, I love this gig," Gabriel said as he stared at the most expensive watercraft ever created.

Carly was a bit more cautious than Gabriel. "It's too bad we can't send the sub in without this surface work," she said. "I don't like being exposed any longer than we have to."

Dash agreed, but they all knew the limitations of the technology. STEAM 6000 had made sure to explain it in excruciating detail and test them relentlessly while they were in Gamma Speed. They would need to ride the surface of the water and search for an oily film of Pollen Slither. Once they found that, they could trace a direct path to the origin twenty thousand feet below.

"Sure would be nice if we could just scoop up some Pollen Slither from the surface and use that," Carly continued while they all put on life vests and boarded their own watercrafts.

"No way!" Gabriel said. "All that training on the ship with these things. We've gotta ride 'em for real."

Dash knew he should reassure Carly, but he could

feel himself being pulled into the gravitational force of Gabriel's excitement.

"I'm not going to lie. I've been looking forward to this."

"That's my man," Gabriel said, and he leaned out for a fist bump that Dash neglected to see.

"Don't leave me hangin'," Gabriel said.

Dash returned the bump, then shifted to his left, where Carly was seated, and offered a fist bump to her. She took a deep, nervous breath and put on her helmet, ignoring Dash's fist. "Let's do this."

Dash and Gabriel put on their helmets, and everyone buckled into their seats.

"Ready?" Dash asked, testing the person-to-person audio inside the helmets. He got nods all around and tapped a command into his screen. "Piper, open bay doors."

"You got it," Piper said from the deck. A hydraulic sound filled the *Cloud Cat* bay and light pierced Dash's eyes. He stared down a forty-five-degree metal ramp, followed by open air and the water below. He tried to swallow and found a lump in his throat that felt like a walnut.

"Gabriel, deploy in five, four, three, two, one," Dash ordered.

Gabriel's watercraft flew down the deck like a stone in a slingshot: it arced up and swayed left, then straightened out and glided onto the surface of the water. Gabriel zoomed away from the ship and circled back, waiting for the rest of his team as he pumped his fist in the air.

"Carly, deploy in five—"

Dash didn't get any further into the order before Carly's watercraft flew out of the cargo bay. She took a sharp right and nearly flipped over, then went into a hard nosedive and pierced the surface, disappearing like a swordfish into the depths of the sea.

"Carly!" Dash yelled. Just as the water started to settle and turn smooth and glassy, Carly's watercraft burst out into the open again, achieved seven feet of amazing air, and landed perfectly on the surface.

Gabriel was super jealous.

"Aw, man, why didn't I think of that," Gabriel said. "Incredible!"

"Thanks," Carly said. The audio on her helmet communication flickered, but she caught the end of what Gabriel was saying. She tried to smile, but she was soaking wet and a little bit shaken up. Then she thought about it: it was kind of a sweet move and she was still breathing! Maybe this mission wasn't going to be so bad after all.

"Deploying now," Dash informed Piper. His finger was on the trigger that would send him hurtling onto an unknown planet. He hoped his landing would be more like Gabriel's than Carly's. "Close bay doors when I'm clear, then move three-quarters of a mile off the surface and hold."

"Understood," Piper said. "And, Dash?"

"Yeah?"

"You're going to do great."

"Thanks, Piper."

Rocket barked his approval as well, and something about his decision to bring Piper along gave Dash the confidence he needed to press his thumb down on the button. He flew a straight path, hardly wobbling at all, and landed softly on the water below. Carly and Gabriel moved into formation beside him, and they all took a moment to gaze out over the endless water.

"We are so far away from home," Dash said.

"It never gets old," Gabriel added.

Carly didn't have any words. Mostly she felt relief—she'd done it. She was on another planet. Finally. A sun from another galaxy shone down on an aquamarine sea. She leaned over and looked into the endless depths, a void that seemed to go on forever.

The water darkened beneath her, and she looked overhead out of habit. Had a cloud drifted by, blotting out the sun? No, there were no clouds in the cobalt-blue sky. When she looked back, it was gone. Or was it? Maybe *all* the water was darker beneath her.

"Did you guys see that?" she asked.

Carly couldn't be sure she'd seen anything, and she was concerned Dash and Gabriel already thought she was being too nervous. Maybe it was a trick of light from the shimmering sun.

"I don't think it was anything," Carly said.

Then she felt something bump against the bottom of her watercraft.

Dash looked to the sky, hoping to see the *Cloud Cat* still holding low to the water, but it was long gone. There was no time to call Piper back and complete the not-so-simple reboarding procedure. The water swelled up beneath him, like a blue whale was about to crest the surface. He felt his watercraft tilt to one side.

"Evacuate protocol one!" Dash yelled.

They'd practiced two types of evacuation plans during training. One meant stay together; two would have meant split apart and go in different directions. It had taken all of a few seconds on Aqua Gen to stumble into *something*.

"Predator Z!" Dash yelled as he went straight to full throttle and the watercraft bucked and swayed beneath him. He looked back as the surface boiled higher, with Carly and Gabriel on the other side of the creature that was about to show itself.

Dash hoped his team had heard the order through

the helmet comm system, but as the Predator Z broke the surface, he couldn't be sure. It was like nothing Dash had ever seen or imagined, twice as big as a killer whale but so much faster. The length of its entire body flew into the air like a dolphin, dripping water beneath its great hull of a stomach. It was the most amazing bright blue color, which only made the rows of teeth stand out more. Dash turned hard to the right, trying desperately to outrun the tidal wave the Predator Z created. A twenty-foot wall of water rose up behind him, pushing Dash faster and faster. The normal top speed of the watercraft was somewhere in the neighborhood of forty-five miles per hour, but the wave pushed his speed to sixty. He was literally flying along the surface, barely holding on.

Dash looked over one shoulder and then the other, but all he could see was a wall of water. He turned the watercraft softly to his left and began a wide angle against the wave, preparing to rise up and over the cresting water, back toward Gabriel and Carly, he hoped. That was when he saw the Predator Z once more, its lizard-like skin just beneath the surface. It was moving as fast as Dash was, tracking him with a basketball-sized eyeball. A lightning bolt of fear shot through his body as he throttled the watercraft to full speed, pulling away from the menacing eyeball. The beast moved in behind Dash and took chase as Dash turned hard into the open sea and crouched down, creating the best airstream he could.

"Show me what you've got," he said as he hit the watercraft's accelerator to speed up to seventy miles per hour. He'd seen footage of speedboats catching the wrong angle and going airborne, tumbling end over end and breaking into pieces. One wrong move and the same fate awaited Dash, and then he'd be Predator Z food for sure. The water lay like an endless sheet of glass in front of him, and he glided along its surface in a perfectly straight line. A full minute passed, and he didn't look back. It felt like he could go on like this forever in search of a distant shore and never find one.

At last, he risked lifting his head and turning around, expecting to see the great alien creature of the sea bearing down on him. Instead he saw only the line on the water he'd left behind, like the third-base line to home. He throttled down and turned in the direction from which he'd come, then came to a stop, bobbing gently on the water.

"Where are you?" he whispered to himself, searching every corner of the horizon.

Dash doubled back in search of his teammates and hoped they hadn't been capsized. He saw nothing. No Predator Z. No Carly or Gabriel. He drove the watercraft in a circle, feeling a sudden loss of direction. Everything looked the same. Water, water, and more water.

"Carly! Gabriel!" he called out. The quiet unnerved him. He felt a loneliness he hadn't experienced for weeks. On his second spin around, Dash saw the Predator Z rise once more, about a hundred yards to his left. It was cutting a path in the distance, and he felt a pang of hysteria at the idea that one or both of his friends were clutched between its teeth.

Dash double-checked the helmet communication system and tried again.

"Gabriel, come in! Carly, answer!"

Dead air. Dash changed frequencies. Then he tried switching to his MTB. Still no word from Carly or Gabriel.

"Piper, come in!"

A few seconds of silence followed, then Piper's voice came through. "Piper here."

"We've been separated," Dash said. "But all three watercraft have GPS signals. Where are they?"

"Checking," Piper said. "I'm out of Aqua Gen's atmosphere, but I can return if you need me to. Sounds like things are off to a rocky start."

Dash thought about it. He remembered the briefing; the last thing they needed was the AquaGens discovering they'd been visited by humans from another galaxy.

"Hold your position. Any sign of Carly or Gabriel?"

"Okay. Yeah, I have them both. I also see your signal. They're together, due east. Not moving. At top speed, I'd say you're three minutes away."

"Try to hail them. I'm on the move," Dash said.

He throttled the watercraft and headed east, pushing the machine as hard as it would go. A minute passed as water sprayed up on both sides, then another. Piper's voice returned.

"No answer from Carly or Gabriel. I'm coming down there."

"Stay put!" Dash ordered. "I'm almost there. We can't risk another *Cloud Cat* entry already. Give me another minute or two."

Dash was back at over sixty miles per hour in no time flat, following Piper's instructions from above.

"A little more to the north—you're off course," Piper explained.

Dash adjusted his direction too quickly and began to fishtail across the surface. He was losing control of the watercraft. Throttling down slowed his weaving back and forth, and he was able to steady himself. A few more seconds and Dash saw two dots on the water in the distance. He couldn't tell if they were carrying his friends or not, but at least he'd found the watercraft.

"Come on, guys. You have to be there."

A minute later, the two watercraft began to move toward Dash and he knew—he and his crew had found each other. They were okay.

"I have them," Dash said on Piper's frequency. "We're good. Just a little brush with a Predator Z."

"That took all of four seconds," Piper said. "I hope it's not a sign of bad things to come."

Gabriel broke out in a smile as he and Carly approached Dash, and the three of them did some whooping and hollering.

"Nothing the Alphas can't handle," Gabriel said triumphantly.

"You had us worried," Carly said, searching the surface of Aqua Gen as far as she could see. "It's bigger than I thought it would be."

"Why didn't you answer when I called?" Dash asked. "You can't do that—we're a team!"

Gabriel had heard one of Dash's calls flickering in and out, but hadn't taken it seriously. He thought Dash's nerves were getting the best of him.

"Chill out, Dash," Gabriel said. "We both overturned, totally soaked our helmets and our wrist tech. They're starting to come back online now, but there was no signal for a while there."

Gabriel could tell Dash was already calming down now that he understood what had happened. Besides, he'd worked alongside his friend long enough to trust him even when he was acting kind of like a jerk.

"Mine was already dunked once from the launch," Carly added. "Everything happened so fast. I didn't even realize the audio had shut down."

"That was seriously insane, though," Gabriel said to Dash. "You went down one side, and we went down the other. Predator Z wave is a wild ride!"

Now Dash was smiling. Gabriel's energy was infectious. "I got lost there for a minute," Dash said. "Sorry."

"Forget about it!" Gabriel said. "We're all getting off

this giant swimming pool together. No one gets left behind!"

"What's up down there?" Piper asked from the *Cloud Cat*. She was coming in clear for Dash, but it was a sputtering mess on Carly's and Gabriel's equipment. "I've got my finger on the return to Aqua Gen button."

"We're all fine," Dash called back. "You did a great job, Piper. You got us back together."

"So, do we know where we're going?" Carly asked.

Gabriel nodded. "This Predator Z encounter had one positive outcome. We're closer to a Pollen Slither deposit."

"Point the way, Navigator," Dash said. He gunned the watercraft and did a full circle, like he was riding a dirt bike back home.

"This way," Gabriel confirmed.

He sounded like his usual confident self, but as he led the way, Gabriel began to worry—the radar system pointed them even farther east. They were getting pretty far from their original insertion point. If the radar led them miles and miles away, there was no telling what they might encounter.

Anna scanned the skyline as they flew the *Clipper* a mere ten feet above the water line. It was an agile craft, much smaller than the *Light Blade*, which waited for their return in the atmosphere above.

"Where are you hiding?" Anna wondered aloud, scouting for signs of alien life.

"Why are we doing this again?" Ravi asked as he examined a wide screen of data pouring into view. "Shouldn't we be searching for Pollen Slither?"

"Don't worry about that. Right now I need to find whoever's living in this swamp."

"This is not swamp water," Ravi said. "More like a glacial melt. It's very pure."

Anna rolled her eyes. What she wouldn't give for a crew that didn't question every little thing. As far as she was concerned, they were all too busy proving they were the smartest person in the room to be of much use.

"Wait, I have something," Ravi said.

Anna thought she saw it too: a series of marks on the horizon.

"And we have a lock on the Alpha team position?" she asked.

"Yes, we've had that for a while. Easy to tap into their GPS."

"How far from here are they?"

Ravi did some quick calculations.

"The objects in the distance are approximately seven miles west of us. The Alpha team is due east, about five miles."

The *Clipper* was traveling at over two hundred miles per hour. At that speed, they'd be on top of whatever they were seeing in just over two minutes.

"Okay, time for you to take a break," Anna said.

"A break? What do you mean, break?"

Anna got right up in Ravi's face, leaning down and staring at him sharply.

"I need to navigate this ship. Now."

Ravi knew that look. That determination. He'd seen it at least once every day since they'd left Earth. He'd seen the look as recently as that morning, when she'd waited for him to relay coordinates for their entry point and it had taken a few seconds too long. There was no place for distractions on Anna's Omega team. You either did your job quickly and efficiently, or she did it herself.

And yet Ravi had long ago decided he liked Anna. She was strong and smart, and she could be funny when she really wanted to be. He liked funny. Like when she used withering sarcasm that wasn't pointed at him. "You're not always messing up the orders I give you," she'd said to Siena a few days before. "Sometimes you're asleep." Siena had it the worst—she was second-in-command, a possible threat to Anna's hold on power.

But there were times, such as the moment he found himself in now, when Anna truly scared him. Ravi got up and moved off.

"You might want to buckle up," Anna said. "This could get a little bumpy."

Ravi knew better than to take an order like that lightly. He switched seats with her and secured himself for whatever Armageddon was about to happen.

"This is good," Dash said, staring at the surface as they waited. They had gone several miles and stopped, waiting for the water to go as calm as possible all around them. But it wasn't turning glassy as it had when they arrived.

"There are clouds moving in," Carly said, staring off into the distance.

Gabriel sniffed the air. He had a keen sense of weather patterns.

"It does smell like rain," Gabriel said as he looked over his shoulder. "It's coming from that way."

"Let's fan out twenty yards apart and start taking readings," Carly said.

The Alpha team spread out, tapping commands into their flat screens. The noses of their watercraft began to hum like vacuum cleaners, sucking up surface film as they checked for density. Carly hoped the resulting data could be analyzed and quickly lead them to the closest source of Pollen Slither.

"Piper, we're going to start sending you data to unpack," Carly relayed the information to the *Cloud Cat.*

"Fire when ready," Piper said. "I'm all set up here."

Piper had scored higher than anyone else on Pollen Slither analysis, the more technical aspect of the challenge. She may have only been 67 percent ready to find the source of Pollen Slither, but she'd scored 99.8 percent on the analysis aspect. Carly was a data hound too, and she knew a fellow analysis geek when she saw one. Piper's score was second only to STEAM 6000, who had been perfect.

They spent the next five minutes sucking up a film of Pollen Slither and gathering information.

"That should be plenty," Carly said as she rode a circle past her two teammates. "There are hundreds of Pollen Slither mines at the bottom of all this water. We just need to find one."

Carly gathered up the data and uploaded it to Piper. A few seconds later, Piper responded. "All systems go here. Looks like the mapping will take a while."

"How long?" Carly asked.

"Several hours, possibly longer. It's hard to tell for sure."

A collective *ugh* registered from Dash, Carly, and Gabriel.

"Should I come down and get you guys?" Piper asked.

"Negative," Dash replied. "Just keep us posted."

Piper signed off at the same moment Carly spotted something on the horizon.

"The wind is picking up," Gabriel said as his water-craft bobbed up and down against small whitecaps. "Maybe we should get out of here for now?"

"I'm not sure how easy it will be to get the *Cloud Cat* in position if we find ourselves in a real windstorm," Dash agreed.

"What do you suppose that is?" Carly asked, ignoring the boys' comments. Something off in the distance seemed to be heading their way.

Gabriel and Dash turned to look as Carly moved in closer to Gabriel's watercraft.

"Gabe, try the magnifying goggles."

Gabriel opened a small compartment on his water-craft and took out a pair of high-powered binoculars. The device was small and silver, and when Gabriel turned it on, a circle of green lights lit up around the lenses. He brought the device to his eyes.

"It's getting closer," Carly said. "Let's get Piper down here."

"No, wait," Gabriel said. "You guys aren't going to believe this."

He set the device in his lap and shook his head.

"It's the *Clipper.* The Omega team is heading right for us, very low to the water."

"No way," Dash said. "They're trying to piggyback on our discovery."

"Jerks," Carly said. "Why don't they find their own Pollen Slither mine?"

Gabriel was looking through the device again as a gust of wind blasted them all in the face. As soon as it arrived, it was gone.

"Whoa, that was some breeze," Carly said.

"You guys," Gabriel said. The tone of his voice had changed.

"I see it," Dash said.

"Omega is creating a Predator Z–sized wake. They're blasting right on the surface of the water!"

"Go, go, go!" Carly yelled. She punched the water-craft into gear, but she knew it was too little too late. The Omega *Clipper* was traveling way faster than she and her teammates could. It was bearing down on them like a destroyer, building a wall of water on both sides that rose forty feet into the air.

"We can't outrun them!" Gabriel yelled. "We need to split up!"

"No! Let's stick together this time," Dash insisted. "They're not going to run us down. No way would they do that. They're just trying to scare us off our find. Let's make a wide turn and circle back toward them!"

"What?" Carly yelled. "Why would we do that?"

Dash turned hard, a look of fierce determination on his face. "'Cause we're not running from Omega. Not today."

Gabriel let out a rebel yell and followed, a huge smile on his face. "That's my man!"

As they made their turn, Carly followed Dash, who was going wider still so they could get a better look at what they were dealing with. The Omega *Clipper* was now within twenty seconds or so of catching them, and Carly was sure Anna or whoever was in control would come up short or turn sharply away.

And she was almost right.

The *Clipper* didn't turn or stop, but it did change course, suddenly bursting off the water and straight up into the air. A moment later, it was far enough into the sky that Carly could hardly see it.

They all stopped as the wave died down and sent them up and down on a long, rocking wake of twenty feet or so.

Gabriel let off a few choice words, but Dash had turned white as a ghost.

"I can't believe they'd be that reckless," Carly said. "They could have really hurt one of us."

Dash shook his head. "They weren't trying to hurt us. They were leading someone *toward* us."

"Huh?" Gabriel said. He followed Dash's gaze. So did Carly.

An armada of alien sea ships was coming right toward them.

"I guess this means we won't be going with Plan A," Gabriel said.

"What was Plan A again?" Carly asked.

"Keeping a low profile," Dash said as his mind raced with options, none of which made any sense. They could try to outrun a fleet of alien ships, but that would never work. They could call in Piper, but that would probably only make things worse. They had only one choice, and he knew it. "We'll have to make contact."

Gabriel shook his head like he couldn't believe how messed up things had gotten. "I hope they're not pirates. That would be a seriously bad deal."

"Chris told us in the briefing the AquaGens were an advanced race with a language all their own," Dash reminded them. He looked at Carly. "You have the translator?"

Carly nodded and patted a zipped-up pocket on her suit.

"Everyone stay calm," Dash said.

The ships were slowing down as they approached, and

this gave the Alpha team a look at what they were dealing with. Six massive vessels, each with more sails than any of the Alphas had ever seen on a single ship. The sails were iridescent, casting a weird green-and-blue shimmer as they flapped in the wind. More and more of them were being rolled down, cutting speed as they approached.

The ships themselves were like something out of a future Earth. They were part metal, part wood, with wide brass tubing that seemed to hold everything together like thick rope. Long, needlelike noses extended from the fronts of each ship, like spears ready to cut through whatever lay in their path.

"I'm going to say this one more time, just because," Gabriel said. "I really hope these aren't zombie pirate ships."

Carly nodded. "Me too."

When the ships were fifty yards away, they spread out, encircling the Alpha team. A sound like a gun went off, an air blast that pierced Dash's ears.

"Stay calm," Dash said. "They're not firing on us."

At the sound of the blast, a cable of some kind had unfurled across the open water, sending a line from one ship's deck to another.

It was then that Carly saw several of the crew members for the first time. They were clothed entirely in blue from head to toe. Even their faces were covered. Whatever the fabric was, it looked almost liquid from a distance.

One of the blue-clad sailors climbed the tallest mast

like a monkey and attached the cable. This made the line across the gap in the water go from high to low, one end on either ship.

Several sailors climbed the same mast and arrived at the top, staring down at the Voyagers with eyes Carly couldn't see. They seemed to be awaiting a signal.

A voice broke through the wind, speaking in a language Carly had no knowledge of.

"They're asking us something," Carly said. "Hang on."

She pulled a phone-sized tablet from her waterproof pocket. Carly was the best linguist the Voyagers had, and she'd been waiting for this to come up: a language barrier between two intelligent peoples.

The voice boomed over the water again.

"It sounds like a dolphin gargling mouthwash," Gabriel said flatly.

"Got it that time!" Carly said, her fingers flying across the screen. "Just another second and I can translate."

"Really?" Gabriel asked.

"Really," Carly confirmed. The device was one of a kind, made by the ZRKs with Chris's help. Carly had recorded the gurgling voice, and now the translator was busy cracking the code on whatever the language was.

Carly tapped a command on the small screen and put her mouth next to one end. And then she yelled.

"We come in peace! We mean you no harm!"

A few seconds later, the same gurgling dolphin sound blasted out of the translator.

"Good job, Carly," Dash said. "What did they say before?"

"The first message was *Don't move.* The second message: *These are infested waters.*"

"Infested? What does that mean?" Gabriel asked, pulling his feet up closer to his chest and peering into the water.

The voice rose up again, weird and watery.

"What did it say?" Dash asked.

Carly had set the translator into automatic mode, and a second later, the device answered Dash's question with the voice of a British female.

"We're coming to get you. Stay still."

Gabriel's eyebrows went up. "They sound nice."

"It's only a setting on the translator. I could use the 'burly truck driver' setting if you'd prefer," Carly replied.

"No, I like the nice English lady," Gabriel said. "Keep it."

Dash told Carly to ask another question.

"What are these waters infested with?"

The translator did its work and an answer came back.

"Thermites and sea monsters we call Predator Zs."

Gabriel gulped. "This just gets better and better."

Dash did his best to project calm and confidence. "They won't hurt us," he said. "We're not armed and dangerous. This will be okay."

Another message was translated: "We will come get you, but those machines you're riding will have to stay. They have no place here. Stand up."

"Stand up?" Carly wondered.

The voice came once more: "Hurry. We need to get you out of the water. Now."

Three sailors jumped from the highest point of the mast and slid down the cable like a zip line, each of them holding a hand toward the water.

"I think they want us to go with them," Dash said. He stood up, wobbling back and forth on his watercraft. "Come on, you guys."

"We could still make a run for it," Gabriel said. "You sure about this?"

"I'm sure," Dash said. He was anything but.

As the blue-clad sailors glided down the cable, Dash felt the water under him begin to rise. He looked down and saw the sea bubbling up around the watercraft. And something else, something bad.

His water suit was punctured on his lower left leg, and out of the hole a bright red substance was leaking. How did that happen? Dash thought through everything that Chris had told them, and his mind seized on one fact: *Predator Z is highly attracted to blood. Do NOT bleed into the water on Aqua Gen. Ever.*

"You guys," Dash said.

Carly and Gabriel could hear the concern in Dash's voice as they turned and looked at him.

"I'm bleeding," Dash informed them. "I must have cut myself when the Predator Z came through."

The surface started to bubble even more, like they

were in a kettle of boiling water, and Dash heard the strange voice of the sailors once more. It was only one word, and when it was translated, he obeyed.

"JUMP!"

The AquaGens had arrived overhead on the zip line.

Dash, Carly, and Gabriel leapt into the air, grabbing outstretched hands as they swung by, and not a second too soon. The water split open like a great furnace of fire, and a Predator Z emerged. As it rose, the creature scooped all three watercraft into its mouth, the jagged teeth ripping through cable as it moved clean out of the sea. Its head jerked back and forth like a dog with a toy, and it turned, facing the water once more, slamming down and vanishing into the deep.

The cable suddenly snapped. Gabriel, Dash, and Carly all shrieked as they swung back toward one of the ships. Holding tight to what was left of the cable, the AquaGen sailors and the Voyagers were plunged into the churning water.

Dash surfaced, gasping for breath. He met Gabriel and Carly's eyes briefly when it dawned on him—they were in the water with a Predator Z and Dash was bleeding! But before panic could set in, they felt themselves being hauled out of the water and toward the ship. Looking up, Dash saw the AquaGens aboard rapidly pulling the cable in. With a sigh of relief, he, Gabriel, and Carly were pulled into the cargo hold, shafts of light pouring in from every side.

The gurgling voices returned as the three sailors pushed Dash, Carly, and Gabriel toward a brass pole leading through a hole into the guts of the ship.

Carly had deposited the translator in a waterproof pocket at her chest. It was safe. She reached for it, and one of the blue-clad sailors made an alarming, high-pitched noise.

"Okay, okay," Carly said. "No worries. You want us to go down there, we'll go down there."

Gabriel glared at Dash. "Dude, this is really not going as planned."

Dash felt awful. Should they have run? Or called Piper in to get them? He watched as Gabriel and then Carly slid down what was basically a fire-station pole.

Dash looked at his captors. "Listen, I can explain. We're not here to do anything bad."

One of the sailors shoved Dash closer to the hole. He wished he could see their faces under those weird iridescent coverings. Just before he slid down the pole, he noticed that their clothing didn't appear to be wet at all.

Down into the depths of the ship Dash went, farther than he expected to.

He'd let his crew get captured by an unknown force.

And now it looked like they were being imprisoned in some kind of seafaring dungeon.

It was an all-time low.

Piper was beginning to freak out.

"Dash? Come in, Dash! Where are you guys?"

She'd been trying to hail Dash or anyone else on the extraction team for over an hour, but she was having no luck.

"Why aren't they answering?" Piper asked herself. Or maybe she had asked Rocket, who sat staring at her with a sort of concerned golden retriever look on his face.

"I don't know what I'm supposed to do, Rocket. What if they're in real trouble?"

Rocket moved his head closer, the soft golden fur touching Piper's cheek. He nuzzled under her chin and stayed there while Piper quietly let her hand fall on the dog's side.

"It's okay, boy. We're going to get through this. And then we all get to go home."

She pulled the dog's face close to her own, the two of them touching foreheads.

"I'm very glad you're here with me," she said, ruffling the dog's fur. Let's get you a treat."

Rocket bounded around the ship like a very big rabbit at the sound of the word *treat* and Piper hovered over to a cabinet and opened it. She reached inside and took out a prefabricated cardboard-looking dog bone.

"Gross," she said. But when she tossed it to Rocket, he might as well have been in heaven. Fake bones were fine by him.

He settled onto the floor, and Piper went back to the control deck at the front of the ship, where the extraction mapping was in progress.

It was cool the way it worked, in stages so she knew exactly how far the calculations had to go. The ship's onboard system was taking the data the Alpha team had gathered and was turning it into a 3-D hologram she could spin and review in the air. It showed the surface area where the Pollen Slither had been found, along with hundreds of tiny tendrils swirling downward into a representation of the sea. They were like the stringy tentacles of a jellyfish, merging with one another as they went deeper and deeper toward their source. Where there were once a hundred or more tendrils, there were now only a dozen. The blue-toned hologram map was about a foot in diameter, and more than ten feet tall from floor to surface. So far, the mapping had only filled in the top foot of the whole, leaving a lot of solid blue still to fill in.

Piper did some calculations.

"Well, Rocket. Looks like we have some time to kill. Like sixteen hours."

She looked out across the vast emptiness of the planet far below and suddenly felt very tired. The sun was dipping toward the horizon, if it could be called a sun at all. The closer it got to going down, the bluer it became.

"It's beautiful."

Piper floated her air chair to the deck again, and Rocket came over, laying his head in her lap.

"STEAM 6000 here," a voice crackled into the *Cloud Cat*. "Status update?"

Piper didn't know what else to say, so she told the truth. She always did.

"I've lost contact with the extraction team. What should I do?"

A pause, but only briefly. "Dash knows what he's doing. He will be fine."

"Should we try to hail Shawn or ask Chris what he thinks?"

Another pause, longer this time.

"I have just tried Earth four thousand seven hundred and twelve times. We're not getting through."

"What about Chris?"

"I'm afraid he's otherwise occupied. He's in the middle of a recalibration of TULIP's processors. It's delicate work that requires his complete concentration.

If he stops, he'll have to start over. That would be ill advised."

"Okay . . . if you say so."

"TULIP must be reprogrammed before we reenter Gamma Speed. We can't afford to start over now."

"What's the big rush?" Piper asked.

There was another long pause.

"I follow the chain of command," STEAM said. "Dash Conroy has ordered me to keep Chris focused on this important task."

"But why do we need to leave Aqua Gen so quickly? Why couldn't we stay on an extra day or two?"

Piper waited for a few seconds while STEAM didn't answer her.

"STEAM? Are you there?"

A few more seconds passed before STEAM responded.

"I'm not authorized to discuss the medical condition of Alpha team participants."

And with that, STEAM was gone.

Piper looked at Rocket.

What was STEAM talking about? Piper was the ship's medic, and she hadn't been told about a medical issue. She let that idea roll around in her head like a marble, and then tried Dash once more.

No answer.

The sun went down, a whole day gone, and darkness enveloped the watery world of Aqua Gen.

When Anna entered the bridge of the *Light Blade*, she immediately felt the icy temperature in the room. So, word of her recent piloting work on Aqua Gen had gotten back to them already. She glared at Ravi, who quickly passed by and sat in his usual spot. He wouldn't make eye contact with her. None of them would.

If her crew thought they could take her down a notch by ganging up on her, they were wrong. They'd never met her dad, a taskmaster extraordinaire with a penchant for emotional and mental trickery. Ravi, Siena, and Niko had nothing on the master manipulator known as Mr. Turner. She'd learned the craft of holding the upper hand from the best of them.

Anna strode down the center of the observation deck, putting off an icy coldness of her own.

"Siena?" she asked, all business. "What's the status on element retrieval mapping?"

Siena didn't respond to the request. She didn't even look up.

"All right," Anna said. "I'll take your silence to mean you've fallen behind the allotted time. I'll have Colin do it. You are relieved of duty for now."

"But—" Siena blurted out.

"Do you have results for me or don't you?" Anna broke in. "Because Colin can do it if you can't. Am I wrong about this, Colin?"

Colin had enough brains to do almost any task on the ship. He felt, deep in the coldness of his beating heart, that it was he who was really in charge of the *Light Blade* and the mission. These kids were nothing but a set of tools he used to attain his ultimate goal: showing Ike Phillips that he was better than the alien he'd been cloned from. His greatest ally was Anna, but eventually he would need to show her how inferior she was. For now, he played along.

"You are correct."

Colin's cold words rattled Siena even more.

"There, you see?" Anna said. "We don't exactly need you, Siena. There are others on this team who can do the work if you can't."

"Ravi told us what you did," Siena shot back, looking at her wrist tech and bringing up a series of messages Ravi had typed in.

Anna is taking us in close to a fleet of Aqua Gen ships. . . .

They're taking chase!

You guys, she led them right to the Alpha team.

This isn't right.

Anna glowered at Ravi once more.

"Do you deny it?" Siena asked.

Niko and Ravi looked on with nervous curiosity. Colin smiled. He loved nothing more than seeing the Omega team turn on itself.

"We told you, Anna," Niko said. "We don't want anyone to get hurt. Not on our team or theirs."

"No one is getting hurt," Anna said.

It was time to alter course, Anna knew. She'd threatened Siena's utility on the ship, that seed had been planted. Now she must turn them in her direction.

"No one is getting hurt," Anna repeated. "You read the reports just as I did. The AquaGens are a peaceful people. They're not going to hurt anyone, but they will detain them and slow them down. Aren't you tired of being told we're second best? If you're not, there's the door. Go join them. None of us were chosen, and we all should have been. We're a better team. We deserve to lead. We deserve to be heroes. And they took that from us."

She could see by the looks on their faces that she was winning them over. They wanted out from under the Alpha shadow as much as she did.

"You have to trust me. I'm not going to do anything that will get anyone hurt, not on their team and certainly not on ours. What I *am* going to do is lead this team. I'm going to make sure Earth gets what it needs. Because ultimately, I don't think the Alpha team is up to the task. If we don't get them out of the way, they'll blow the whole thing, and do you know what that means? No energy source. And no going home."

Anna sat down in her captain's chair and stared out into the stars. "I'm the best shot you've got."

Niko was the quietest of the group, but he spoke next.

"You're forgetting something, Anna. You need us as much as we need you."

Anna didn't like having to count on anyone. Niko's words stung more than they should have, because he was right. As much as she wished she could, Anna couldn't beat the Alpha team alone. Her mind seized on the right course of action: *They need to think I actually care about them. They need to think they matter.* She turned to look at her crew.

"You're right, Niko. I do need you guys." She gulped a big breath and faked the part of contrite leader. "I should have asked you all about the plan first. I shouldn't have made that decision alone. I'm sorry."

Inside, Anna wanted to scream. She wanted to tell them to grow up and do their jobs. But she held her ground even as her hands were shaking with anger.

"Did the universe just do a backflip or was that Anna Turner saying she was wrong?" Ravi joked.

"Don't get used to it," Anna said. She turned her captain's chair to stare out at the stars once more, signaling that this conversation was over.

"Take back what you said," Siena insisted. She had never once failed a task, no matter how demeaning. Anna could hear the venom in her voice. Siena wasn't done fighting, not by a long shot.

Anna wanted to tell Siena to leave the bridge. She wanted to humiliate her. But she held herself in check.

"I *meant* what I said, Siena. If you choose not to do your job, someone else can do it. But there's no question in my mind that you are the most qualified for the task I gave you. I would not have assigned it to you if I didn't think you were the most talented person for the job."

"I think that was an apology, sort of," Niko said. Mostly he just wanted everyone to get along.

Siena sat back down at her station and tapped out a few commands on the glass before her.

"We're going to talk about some of these tactics at some point too," Siena said. They were right on the edge of what she was comfortable with, and it had been happening more and more.

"But now's not the time," Niko said, nodding and raising an eye at Siena as if to say "You've already gotten as much as you're going to get today. Don't push it."

"We're hacked in," Sienna said. "Everything is working as planned. Now all we can do is wait."

Anna sat in her commander's chair and felt a mix of emotions. She wished she hadn't been forced to fake an apology to anyone. But it *had* gotten the desired effect from her crew. She was beginning to wonder, *Maybe there's more to leading than my dad taught me.*

Only time would tell.

Piper's head had lolled to one side on the backrest of her air chair. A bead of slobber was rolling down her cheek. She was a heavy sleeper, always had been, and when sleep came, it was hard to rouse her. Rocket heard a very small noise from the control panel and lifted his head off his paws. But he didn't stir any more than that, and a moment later, his eyes closed again.

Even if Piper had been awake, she wouldn't have understood the *Cloud Cat* system was being hacked into by the Omega team. STEAM 6000 would have noticed. The Alpha robot would have put up a defense or alerted someone. But Piper knew only the rudimentary controls of the *Cloud Cat*. She knew how to tell it what to do and let auto settings do the rest. She was primarily a doctor.

The Omega team wouldn't fall behind because Anna revealed the Alpha team's position to the AquaGens. Team Omega would crack the code for finding the Pollen Slither source as fast as the Alpha team would. And once that happened, they'd have a serious leg up.

Dash was sitting inside the belly of an Aqua Gen sailing vessel, thinking about everything that had gone wrong. As the ship lolled back and forth on the water, he was silently freaking out. He'd listened to Carly and Gabriel yell for help for a long time, but after a while, they gave up and sat down on the cold floor of the ship. An hour later, they had both fallen asleep. But Dash remained wide awake, cycling through the list of problems that needed solving:

- The AquaGens had taken all their communication devices, so Dash had lost contact with Piper and the *Cloud Cat*. He had no idea where she was or how she was doing. He hoped she hadn't chosen to come looking for them.
- His team was trapped inside an alien ship with no apparent way to escape and the clock was ticking.
- Speaking of clocks, Dash had no idea what time it was. He thought it was getting close to morning,

but he couldn't be sure. He hadn't planned for an extended stay on Aqua Gen, so he hadn't brought a shot of his elixir with him. What if they got stuck on this planet for more than twenty-four hours?

- The AquaGens didn't trust Dash or his team, and he had no idea how to change their minds.
- And most troubling of all, a sound like nothing he'd ever heard in his life had begun. It was both terrifying and weird. All around him there was a growing reverberation of teeth biting against wood. Not one set of teeth, but many. *Thousands.*

"Hey, wake up, you two," Dash said, nudging Gabriel and Carly awake.

"How long were we out?" Carly asked as she rubbed the sleep out of her eyes.

"Couldn't tell you," Dash offered. "They took all our tech."

Carly felt along her lanky arm and remembered how they'd removed her MTB. She felt naked without it.

"Man, I got used to that thing," Gabriel said, touching his own wrist.

"What's that awful noise?" Carly asked, her face souring like she'd swallowed a bad pickle.

"I hate to tell you guys," Dash said. "But I think this boat is being attacked by a school of—"

He didn't finish, as a door opened at the top of

the winding metal stairway and the room was illuminated with watery light. Dash looked at the ceiling and saw that it was shimmering with color, not unlike the Pollen Slither he'd seen on the surface of the sea. It was casting a soft glow on the room. *Pollen Slither must be some powerful stuff,* he thought. It was what they'd used to make the iridescent sails on the ships and probably so much more.

Down the stairs came three AquaGens, all hidden behind the same flowing fabric, the arms and legs fluttering like waves. One, presumably the leader, also wore a silver band around his or her forehead.

When they arrived at the bottom of the stairs, the leader tossed the translator to Carly and nodded.

"Looks like they're ready to talk," Dash said.

Carly quickly turned the device on.

"Tell him he's got a nice place here," Gabriel said.

"Gabriel, this is no time for jokes," Carly said, shoving him in the shoulder and giving him a look.

"You have led us into dangerous waters," the Aqua-Gen leader said. It came out all gurgles and squeaks, but the translator turned it into that reassuring female British voice. "We had hoped to avoid Thermites, but we have not. Come with us. It's not safe here any longer."

The sound of a million teeth biting at the hull brought the training images into Dash's mind. Each Thermite was up to twenty feet long, with suction cups like an octopus filled with thousands of sharp teeth.

"How many are there?" Dash asked.

One of the AquaGens at the leader's side unsheathed a blade that looked like a samurai sword and moved in Dash's direction.

Gabriel couldn't help himself: "Was it something we said?"

Dash pushed his teammates back, blocking them from the oncoming threat.

"We come in peace!" Dash said, repeating a line they'd already tried and failed to get much use out of.

"Stand aside," the blade-wielding AquaGen gurgled as he strode past the Voyagers.

The sound of teeth biting at the hull was coming from every corner of the room, growing in volume.

"To the deck!" the leader yelled. "Now!"

Dash pushed Carly and Gabriel forward and followed as quickly as he could. He heard a new sound, like water exploding through a fire hose, and turned back.

A Thermite tentacle had breached the hull, thrashing three feet in the air through the hole, searching for something else to sink its teeth into. The AquaGen moved quickly, slicing the sword through the air and cutting the tentacle clean about a foot above the hole. The lopped-off section flailed around like a fish out of water and what remained of the Thermite arm retracted. Water began pouring in through the hole. Seconds later, a second Thermite broke through. Then a third. Then they were breaking through the wooden underbelly of the ship like popcorn in a microwave.

"Run!" the AquaGen leader shrieked, pushing Dash up the staircase.

As he came around the second turn of the spiral, Dash glanced down once more. The two AquaGens who remained were both mowing down Thermite tentacles as fast as they appeared, but this only seemed to hasten the demise of the ship. They were taking on water fast.

"Enough!" the leader yelled at the crew. "There's nothing left to be done. We must abandon ship."

"I'm sorry," Dash said, and while he couldn't see the captain's eyes, he did catch the smallest head nod under the mask of watery fabric.

When they reached the deck, the sun was just coming up over the dome of Aqua Gen. There were three ships stationed nearby in a cluster about a hundred yards off. Everything was cast in light and shadow as Dash pulled Gabriel and Carly together. "Whatever happens, stay close to each other."

There were a dozen or more AquaGens on the deck, all of them working feverishly at tearing down the sails and rolling them up into tidy bundles. They were much thinner than Dash expected, like wet rice paper pulled from a pot of boiling water.

"Why are they taking down the sails?" Carly asked.

"Yeah, we should be hoisting them so we can make a run for it," Gabriel added.

Dash shook his head. "There's no saving this ship. The sails must be the most valuable asset they have."

Carly and Gabriel stood at the rail and looked down.

"This is so bad," Carly said, her voice cracking with fear. She nervously pulled her black hair back into a ponytail and tied it off with a rubber band.

Dash looked over the edge of the boat too. The water was churning with Thermites. Thousands of them thrashing the surface of the water. How many more were attacking the ship itself?

The captain of the ship came up beside them and spoke.

"Do as we do or die by the teeth of these vile creatures."

The captain moved off quickly, gurgling orders at its crew.

"Wait!" Dash said. He touched the captain's arm but quickly pulled his hand back. The cloth felt like a pool of water.

The AquaGen turned and tilted its head.

"Where are the things you've taken from us?" Dash asked. "They're very important." Without their wrist tech, they couldn't contact Piper or the *Cloud Cat.* They might not ever get off the planet.

The captain turned sideways, and Dash saw a small sack hanging from a rope. "I have them. Now do as we do!"

Dash was glad to hear they hadn't lost their communication to the outside world, but he didn't understand what the captain meant.

"There's too much chatter," Carly said, working the screen on the translator. "I can't tell what anyone is saying."

"You guys," Dash said, "they're fitting entire sails inside those small bags."

The AquaGens all had small white bags with ropes they could sling over their heads. The bags were the size of a backpack, but round and bunched at the top in the shape of a teardrop.

"But that's impossible," Carly said. "Those sails are bigger than fifty of my bedsheets back home."

They watched as the last of the sails were rolled and stuffed into bags. What remained was like a grove of trees in winter, the skeletal spines shooting into the air unable to take on wind and forge their escape.

"They're climbing," Gabriel said. "They're all climbing."

Dash and Carly looked up into the series of masts empty of sails and saw that Gabriel was right. As the nose of the ship began to tilt downward and the sound of angry Thermites grew louder still, Dash knew what they had to do.

"Climb!" he yelled. "This ship is going down!"

The three of them were the last ones on the deck. Everyone else had already fled up into the highest reaches of the mainmast and foremast.

Dash hoisted Carly up onto the first rung of the mainmast, and she started to climb. Gabriel was next, and once he was on, he reached his hand back for Dash.

"We're not done yet, buddy. Let's not go down without a fight."

Dash hesitated and took a last look around the ship's deck. If today was going to be his last day, at least it was going to be with his friends on one of the most exciting day of their lives. Dash took Gabriel's hand, and his foot left the deck of the ship.

"Are you guys seeing this?" Carly asked. The sun was far enough up now that the ships in the distance were more visible. One of them had just used what appeared to be an enormous slingshot to fire a cannonball from its deck.

"Like we don't have enough problems already!" Gabriel moaned.

"Are they firing on the Thermites?" Dash wondered out loud.

"I'd say it's a little late for that," Gabriel pondered as he looked down. "The water's cresting the deck. We're about to be Thermite food!"

"Wait," Carly said. She was watching the cannonball as it approached. "It's not shooting cannons. It's something . . . *else*?"

All eyes turned to the ball flying through the air. A long string followed it, stretching thinner and thinner like a rubber band. The ball itself was getting smaller and smaller.

"This is *so* weird," Gabriel said. "Maybe we're still sleeping and this is some kind of fever dream."

They kept watching as Thermites gorged on the ship below.

By the time the ball reached the upper section of the mainmast, far above Carly's head, it was the size of a Ping-Pong ball. The rest of the ball had apparently unwound—a long, stretchy string a hundred yards in length holding it to another ship.

One of the AquaGens reached out his palm and the Ping-Pong–sized ball popped like a bubble with a loud slapping sound. What was left of the ball encircled the AquaGen's hand.

And then, as if by some trick of magic, the AquaGen was flying.

"They have the coolest toys in outer space," Carly said with wonder in her voice.

"Man, none of my friends back home are going to believe this," Gabriel added.

"As if you have friends back home," Carly retorted, making Gabriel laugh.

Watching someone fly across the sky on a super-human rubber band while the ship you were standing on was being devoured? It was something the Alpha team would never be able to fully explain if they ever made it home. It was inspiring and terrifying all at once.

They watched as the AquaGen flew up and over the ship, landing in Thermite-free water by the ships in the distance.

"That looked like a potentially painful landing,"

Gabriel said. "But I'm totally up for it. This is going to be like getting shot from a cannon!"

The balls kept coming, fast and furious, as the ship kept sinking. Every time someone launched off the ship, the Voyagers moved farther up the mainmast. And it was a good thing too, because the only pieces left of the ship *were* the masts. Everything else had been eaten or sunk below the water line.

When only the captain of the ship and the Alpha team remained, the captain called to Dash and his team in a watery voice. The translator was working again now that there weren't so many AquaGens yelling.

"I'll be the last to go," the captain said. "Just put your hand out. They'll shoot right for you."

Dash liked this leader more and more. It knew when it was time to fight and time to run. It had made sure the entire crew was safe before personally trying to escape the danger. And it was going to make sure Dash and his friends, total strangers who had inadvertently lured the AquaGens into a school of Thermites, were safe.

Dash looked up at his crew. "Carly, you next. Then Gabriel."

Carly took a deep breath and tentatively put out her hand as the ship suddenly began to sink much faster. If a Thermite chewed through the two remaining masts, it would be the end of the Alpha team.

Dash heard the loud pop overhead and watched as

Carly flew out into the open air. She sailed over the distant ship, slowed on the other side, and crashed into water he could not see. He hoped she was okay.

"Now you, Gabriel," Dash said, feeling the mast he was on wobble. "Fast!"

"What if it hits me in the face?" Gabriel said.

Dash tried to imagine Gabriel being pulled off the ship's mast by his face, and for some reason, he cracked a smile and shook his head.

"You won't be laughing at my funeral," Gabriel said, and then his outstretched hand produced a giant high-five slap sound and his eyes went wide with fear. A second later, he was pulled out over the water, flying like Peter Pan, screaming and laughing.

Across the way, the foremast leaned precariously toward Dash. It was snapping in two, and the AquaGen captain leapt into the air, landing beside Dash. The translator was with Carly, so Dash wouldn't be able to understand the captain even if he tried.

The mast they stood on began to tip into the water, and Dash looked down, a bad idea. Thermites were whipping the water into a froth of angry teeth. He wouldn't last ten seconds down there.

When Dash looked back at the captain, he was astonished to see that the face covering had been removed. Dash was pretty sure she was a female. She was definitely a strangely kind-looking alien with nearly translucent, extraordinarily white skin. Her face was the same size as an adult human, but her features were very different. Her eyes were twice as big as Dash's and as blue as the sea, domed by long white lashes. Her lips were blue. And long, dark hair fell against high cheekbones.

She smiled and nodded in a reassuring way, and then said something he could not understand. She put out a hand toward his and encircled her fingers around his wrist. Her grip was like iron, strong and sure.

The AquaGen captain dove into the open air and dragged Dash with her as the mast tipped over into the water below. Dash saw the boiling water rise up closer and closer until they were only a few feet away from total disaster. It would come down to this: death on a watery planet, eaten by a sea of alien creatures. At least it would be fast, Dash thought.

He heard but did not see the familiar slap of the ball against skin and felt himself being whisked away on the wind with the force of a gunshot. Dash's legs touched the water, and the slimy tentacle of a Thermite grabbed hold of his shoe. It wrapped quickly around, but Dash was faster still. He kicked hard as they flew, knocking the beast free before it could dig in with its sharp teeth.

As they flew up and over the awaiting ship, Dash looked once more at the captain. They caught eyes for only a moment, and Dash noticed her pale white skin was turning red. She pulled the protective covering over her face and head moments before they hit the water together on the other side.

Their hands separated with the impact, and Dash felt the shock of icy cold on his skin. When he came up for air, bobbing on the water, he saw the two people he most wanted to see in all the world.

"Best ride in the history of rides!" Gabriel howled. "Walt Disney's got nothing on the AquaGen Sling-O-matic!"

Carly just smiled, happy to see her team safe and sound.

They were effortlessly pulled up the side of the ship, where one of the crew members sliced their hands free of the sticky material. The crew on the new ship was covered in the same fabric, and the captain was already busy giving orders. Most of the AquaGens from the previous ship gathered in the middle, but some of them stayed up in the masts and unfurled sails into the sky overhead. There were so many sails Dash couldn't count them all, spread out across four masts that rose into the morning sky.

"She must be the captain of an entire armada of ships, not just one," Dash observed.

"She?" Gabriel asked.

Dash nodded. "She showed me her face. Pretty sure she's a she."

"Was it, you know, gross?" Gabriel asked. "I can only imagine if they talk like a fish they must look like one too."

Dash smiled and shook his head. "Very different looking, but really cool."

"Well, I'm just glad the leader of an entire AquaGen

fleet chose to keep us safe," Carly said. "She must like us at least a little; otherwise she would have left us all to die on that thing."

They turned to the rail and stared out into the distance as the tallest masts of the ship they'd just been on disappeared. The water boiled with Thermites, their gruesome limbs flailing and slapping against the surface of the water. It was hard to watch, especially for Dash.

"She just lost one of her ships," Dash said.

"And saved us," Gabriel reminded him.

They watched as the water became less and less disturbed. The Thermites were under the surface now, tearing the vessel apart as it sank to the bottom of the sea.

Where once there was a commanding AquaGen ship, only a few bubbles remained.

Gabriel stared out into the sea and felt terrible for what had happened. He closed his eyes and hung his head. When he opened his eyes again, he was the first to see that their problems were only just beginning.

"Hey, you guys," Gabriel said. "Who do you suppose that is?"

Dash and Carly followed Gabriel's stare. A man clad in red armor from head to toe was climbing out of the water, up the side of the ship. He looked almost robotic, with a face shielded by mirrored glass and red plates of metal covering his arms, torso, and legs. Metal spikes extended from his armored fingers and feet, and he slammed them into the hull as he continued his ascent. Water dripped from the intruder as he moved slowly and methodically closer.

"This can't be a good thing," Carly said, turning her attention farther down the side of the ship. "Look there."

She pointed to the right, where three more armored men appeared out of the water and began climbing the AquaGen hull.

"This ship is being boarded," Gabriel said as he glanced back and forth between the advancing intruders. He opened his mouth to signal the alarm, but an AquaGen voice boomed from the translator before the words formed on his lips.

"PIRATES!"

Morning broke on the *Cloud Leopard* as STEAM 6000 cycled through a list of details stored in his memory banks. His inner clock told him that Chris still needed an additional nine hours to complete his work on the slogger TULIP. If STEAM interrupted him now, Chris would need to start the whole process over. It would set them back an entire day. And even one day could adversely affect the health of their team leader, Dash Conroy. There was also the very real risk that TULIP could begin leaking, which would effectively end the mission, as alien lava could cut a hole in the ship.

STEAM calculated every outcome of every decision, including his possible decommissioning for having made a catastrophic blunder, and decided to do nothing.

The best STEAM could do was make contact with the *Cloud Cat* and see if Piper had a status update.

Why is the extraction taking so long? What's happening down there?

But STEAM was interrupted by a signal from Earth before he could complete this task.

It was Shawn Phillips, who had finally gotten through. The connection was choppy at best, but STEAM had astonishing language skills, which it used to fill in the dead air and hear the communication as if it were seamless.

"This is Commander Phillips, do you read me?"

The Commander's voice was raspy, as if he'd said those very words a thousand times in a row over the past several hours.

"Connection secure," STEAM 6000 said. "How may I be of service, sir?"

"STEAM! I've been trying to reach you since your scheduled exit from Gamma Speed. Quickly update me in case we're cut off."

STEAM took the next several milliseconds to calculate his answer.

"Extraction of the element Pollen Slither is under way. Chris is conducting important recalibration work on the element housing TULIP."

"Excellent news, STEAM! Well done."

"Thank you, sir."

"How is Dash holding up? And the rest of the team, any problems?"

"I am not aware of any problems, no sir! All is well."

"I seem to have lost the log-file connection. Could you double-check that for me? I haven't seen a ship's log from Dash in quite some time."

"I would be very happy to look into that for you, yes sir."

"Good. And the other team, you didn't lose them, did you? As you know, if they were to get separated from you it would be a catastrophe."

"The *Light Blade* is with us, sir."

There was a longer pause in the connection, and STEAM checked to see if the feed had been lost.

"Sir? Are you there?"

"Yes, I'm here. I didn't expect it to be so difficult, overseeing all of this from so far away."

"We all wish you were here, but I must tell you: the Voyagers you've chosen are getting the job done. You chose correctly, yes sir."

"Thank you, STEAM. Don't forget to get those log files coming again."

"Right away, sir," STEAM replied.

"Signing off, then, for now."

STEAM 6000 moved to the appropriate part of the deck and began working on the broken protocol for sending Dash's log files back to Earth. He was a contented robot, having something important to do, and he neglected to call Piper as he began sifting through millions of lines of computer code.

Siena moved down one of the *Light Blade* hallways in the direction of the SUMI training center. It was there that she would find Anna Turner, conducting additional training in the use of AquaGen submarine technology. On

the way, she had a pang of regret about the information she was about to share. She stopped at one of the many transportation tubes in the ship, tapped out a flight path, and threw herself into the wind tunnel. A few exciting twists and turns later, she was deposited in the library and research lab, housed directly across from SUMI's training center.

She looked both ways down the long corridor and quickly stepped into what passed for a "library" on the ship. She had hoped to find Niko there. Niko loved books—even if there were only a few shabby copies on board. He had told her once, "There's something special about a real book that makes me want to open it." Siena wasn't sure she agreed—she liked her textbooks, sure. But she also liked the immediacy of a computer screen, and the certainty that information was up to date, 100 percent accurate. Besides, "real" books could be read on screens too.

"Can I ask you something?" Siena asked. She had found Niko sitting in a straight-backed chair, hunched over a worn paperback.

To Siena, he had always seemed more boyish than his age—perhaps because he was shorter than the rest of them—while at the same time more mature than he should be. It was a confusing combination that some-times set him apart from the others. He was at once old and young.

"Do you need me on the bridge?" Niko asked, looking up. "I was just taking a short break."

He held up a book and showed its cover, which contained a picture of a blue dragon, and smiled bashfully as if he was really too old for a story about such things.

"I wonder if we'll see dragons before we go home," Siena mused, softening from her usual no-nonsense attitude. "Who knows out here, right?"

"I hope so," Niko replied.

Siena glanced back at the door and brought her voice down to a whisper. Who knew if Colin or SUMI were nearby? Maybe they had superhuman hearing.

"I have it," Siena said in a voice full of uncertainty.

Niko knew what Siena was talking about. "And you're not sure you should give it to Anna? I see your problem."

"I've been thinking about it all night. I mean, it's not technically cheating to steal the coordinates from Alpha so we can get to the element first. It's not like we're in school or playing a game. We're trying to save the world."

Niko closed his eyes and went into one of his "moments." Siena thought of them as micro-meditation sessions. One deep breath, a calm face, and Niko's eyes opened again.

"Anna is our captain," Niko said. "I don't think we stand much of a chance of getting home if there's a mutiny on the ship. For better or worse, she's in charge and we chose to follow her out here."

"So you think I should give her the coordinates, then?"

Niko touched the spine of his book, ran a finger along the edge.

"She's not perfect, Siena. But she's a good captain. She knows what she's doing. It's our job to fall in line with her and do as she says. But there's a line. You know what I mean?"

Siena nodded. This was also very Niko-like. He wouldn't answer a question you needed to answer for yourself. "I need to decide how far I'm willing to go, right? It's my choice."

"It's the same for me and Ravi. We're a team, but we are still individuals. Has Anna crossed a line you can't follow?"

Siena thought of the dangerous game Anna had played on Aqua Gen and the questionable order to hack into the Alpha system.

"I don't think she would intentionally try to hurt anyone," Siena had to admit. "And gathering Alpha data is a strategy that's working for us. If they were smarter, they would have blocked our attempt to access their database. They didn't, and that makes me wonder whether or not they'll be able to complete the mission on their own. But I do think Anna is reckless, and that scares me."

"And her bedside manner is a train wreck," Niko added.

Siena laughed. "If I ever get really sick, I'd rather have Voldemort as my doctor than Anna Turner."

Now they were both laughing.

"I think I have my answer," Siena said. "Thanks, Niko. I owe you one."

Niko nodded and went back to reading his book. He knew it wouldn't be long before the Omega ship would be a blur of activity, getting ready to retrieve the third of six elements to make the Source. Better get in a few more pages of dragon wars while the getting was good.

Colin was in the inner workings of the *Light Blade* with a thousand ZRKs flying around him. Miles of wires and tubes ran between beams of titanium and various motorized parts. It was a complete jumble of machinery, like someone had opened a giant door and flung loads of electronic junk into the innards of the ship. He was firing off commands left and right, sending teams of up to a hundred ZRKs in different directions. They sped away, organized and purposeful.

In here, Colin could safely scream if he wanted to and no one would hear him. He'd certainly done it before. Today, though, he had a lot on his mind.

Colin talked to himself as he worked, a weird habit he'd had for as long as he could remember. He could talk to himself for hours on end.

"Anna Turner this and Anna Turner that. What does he see in her? I'm a hundred times smarter than she is."

Colin sat wedged between two crossbeams, holding a hammer, which he proceeded to slam against a titanium rivet. A pinging echo filled the space, and ZRKs responded with yips and yaps, turning in his direction.

"Go back to work!" Colin yelled.

He resented the ZRKs because they were invented by Chris. *Everything* was invented by Chris. It drove Colin half mad with rage to think of all the things Chris had made. And it made him most upset of all that he himself was really just a copy of the alien. For Colin, Chris was the beginning and end of everything.

"Just once I'd like to make something of my own," he muttered.

He held the hammer up and thought about hitting it against the ship again, but the ZRKs were already behind schedule, and he knew it would set them off. He lowered the hammer and looked around the vastness of the ship, shaking his head.

"If the Omega team knew how unstable this ship was, I wonder what they'd do."

Colin smiled at that idea. The *Light Blade* was barely operational half the time. He and hundreds of thousands of ZRKs had built it in record time because they'd had to. But that had meant cutting a lot of corners.

"They couldn't handle the truth," he realized. "If they knew everything I did, they'd all curl up and hide under their beds. *Including* the unbearable Anna Turner."

Colin couldn't stand how Anna got between him and Ike. He had long since vowed to find a way into the captain's chair.

"If she was out of the way, he would have to make me captain. What else could he do? Ravi and Siena couldn't lead a kid to a toy store. And Niko? *Please.* He's practically useless. There's nothing this crew can do that I can't do better."

Sparks began to fly off to his left, and a bundle of cords broke free from their connection. The wires snaked around the open air shooting electrical charges. One of the ZRKs got caught in the line of fire and ricocheted across the space, bouncing around like a pinball.

Colin opened a panel with a rusty squeak and tapped a few keys inside. The bundle of wire collapsed like a fire hose running out of water and a dozen ZRKs surrounded it.

"Put it back where it belongs, and then I'll turn it on again," Colin said, rolling his eyes. "You guys break more things than you fix."

He knew this wasn't true. Without the ZRKs, the *Light Blade* didn't stand a chance. But he didn't care.

Colin fantasized about Ike seeing all the amazing things Colin could do if he ran the mission. He thought of how little Ike appreciated him.

"How wrong you are about me, Ike Philips. How very wrong."

The AquaGens were in a state of total panic as the first of the pirates reached the rails and leapt onto the deck of the ship. AquaGens were about the same size as humans, but these pirates were something altogether different. Each of them stood between seven and eight feet tall, and with all that red armor, they looked like huge gladiators from the future.

"Still think this is an in-and-out mission?" Carly asked.

"Don't panic," Dash said. "Let's let this play out."

"It's not like we can go anywhere," Gabriel added as he nodded toward the water below. Dash hadn't noticed it in all the commotion, but the wind had really picked up. Angry whitecaps had appeared on the surface of Aqua Gen, rolling the ship in big, sweeping movements.

A total of eight pirates had boarded the ship from different locations, and their massive forms were moving slowly toward the center of the deck.

"What are they saying?" Dash asked.

The pirates were speaking another language than the AquaGens'. It was low and gravelly, full of menace.

Carly fumbled with the translator and almost dropped it as the ship pitched sideways. "I can't lock in on two languages at once. If I try to find a match for these pirates, we'll lose communication with the AquaGens."

"Let's make sure we don't lose the translator completely," Dash said. As bad as things were going, he could imagine the translator flying out of Carly's hand and landing in the water. "Hide it before one of them sees it."

Carly nodded and put the translator back in her pocket.

The captain moved in close behind them and spoke. Her face was covered again like everyone else, and the silver band of steel-like substance encircled her head.

"They won't harm us," she said. "All they want is our treasure. If we let them take it, they'll leave us all alone."

Carly was furious. "Why should these bullies be able to take whatever they want, whenever they want?"

Gabriel agreed, but he was also thinking about how cool red pirates were, even if they were bad guys. He looked at them again."Uh, maybe because these red pirates are eight feet tall and covered in armor?"

Carly rolled her eyes.

"Stay close to me so they put us in the same holding area," said the captain.

"Holding area?" Carly asked. "If this is going to be another Thermite adventure, count me out. I'll stay up here."

"We're on the move for that very reason," the captain said. "To save the ship from the Thermites. Please trust me. Your best chance of survival is to stay with me."

The captain moved off and looked back at the Voyagers. She waved at them to follow. A whispered conversation took place between the captain and another sailor enveloped in blue, and then she was moving again.

"Whoa!" Carly cried. The ship had been moving in a straight line, but it turned hard and Carly's feet went out from under her. She tumbled across the deck and crashed into a sideboard. The same would have happened to Dash and Gabriel, but they'd been lucky enough to grab a railing fast.

"We were almost a couple of bowling pins," Gabriel said.

One of the red pirates moved fluidly across the deck as if the boat wasn't turning sharply at all. It picked up Carly by the shoulders and pulled her back onto her feet, then it grunted something and stared down at her through mirrored glass.

"Hey, leave my friend alone!" Gabriel shouted.

The AquaGen captain put a hand across Gabriel's chest. "Don't provoke them. You won't like where that leads."

The red pirate marched toward the captain, pushing Carly forward. When it arrived at the rest of the group, it spoke in its weird, low voice. The captain responded in a quieter tone that was hard to hear over the crashing waves.

"They understand each other," Carly said with surprise.

Dash hoped they were saying something along the

BASE TEN | PERSONNEL

FIRST NAME	Shawn	**LAST NAME**	Phillips
AGE	37		
GENDER	M		
DATE OF BIRTH	Classified		
NATION OF ORIGIN	United States of America		
ANCESTRY	Son of Ike Phillips, Estranged		
CURRENT OUTPOST	Base Ten, Nevada		
TITLE/POSITION	Commanding Officer, Project Alpha		

STEAM 6000

MAKE/MODEL	Exact Specifications Classified
AGE	Prototype manufactured three years ago
CREW POSITION/TITLE	AI Consultant, Training Robot
CATCHPHRASE	"Yes sir!"

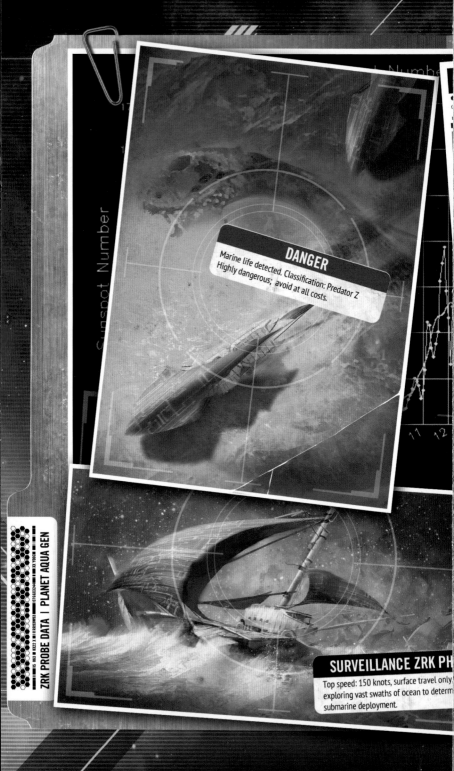

DANGER
Marine life detected. Classification: Predator Z
Highly dangerous; avoid at all costs.

SURVEILLANCE ZRK PH
Top speed: 150 knots, surface travel only
exploring vast swaths of ocean to determ
submarine deployment.

Sunspot Number

11 12

CONFIDENTIAL

DESTINATION: AQUA GEN

This entirely liquid planet requires maneuvering two dangerous realms: the pirate-ridden world that exists above the surface and the treacherous terrain that lurks in the depths of its turbulent seas.

Predicted

NOAA/SWPC

WARNING

PLANET AQUA GEN - Unstable weather conditions.
Reporting extreme wind and heat.

OTO
ideal for
ne

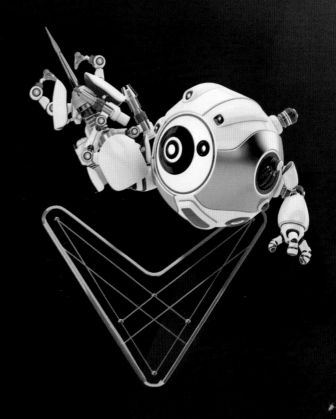

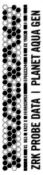

lines of *Let these three kids go back to where they came from,* but somehow he doubted it.

The captain and the red pirate spoke for a long time before the pirate reached for the captain's teardrop-shaped bag, yanking it from her belt. Furious, the captain spouted an angry string of sounds in the pirate's language. The pirate replied calmly, like it was negotiating some sort of peace treaty. The AquaGen captain glared at the pirate but remained silent. Finally, she turned to Dash, Carly, and Gabriel.

"Follow," the captain said.

Gabriel looked across the deck of the ship and saw that some of the AquaGens were being allowed to steer the ship, while others were being herded down into the hull by red pirates. The captain moved forward, then Dash, Carly, and Gabriel followed by the looming red pirate. Dash took Carly's free hand, and Gabriel took Dash's. They stumbled along and came upon a set of stairs leading down. When they arrived at the bottom, there was a narrow shoot of a hallway lined with doors. The red pirate had to turn its massive shoulders sideways and duck its head in order to enter. The captain came to a door and opened it, then stepped aside to let the Voyagers in. They found beds lined three high on both sides. The captain stepped in last, and then a giant red pirate hand pulled the door shut. Gabriel heard other doors shutting from outside as well.

"Obviously they're putting a lot of us down here in rooms to keep us from trying to escape," Dash said.

The captain nodded.

"The red pirate who brought us here will stay in the hallway and make sure we don't try anything. We've been through this before."

"How often?" Carly asked. She felt terrible for the AquaGens. Did they have to deal with an aggressor like this all the time?

"This is the third time they've boarded one of my ships," the captain said. "When we're clear of the Thermite danger, they'll take our sails and go."

"But why do they want the sails?" Carly asked. It all seemed so pointless to her.

"The sails are made of Pollen Slither, and they are very large. They are the most valuable things on the ship."

The boat jostled back and forth, and Gabriel accidentally bumped into Dash, who fell into Carly. All three of them almost ended up on their butts.

"The ship moves very quickly," the captain said. "Stay seated or hold on to something when you stand up."

The Voyagers spilled into the nearest bed and sat together.

"How fast does this thing go?" Gabriel asked. He was keenly interested in the navigational power of alien modes of transportation.

"In this kind of wind? We should exceed a hundred and thirty knots," the captain replied.

"What's the conversion on that, Gabriel?" Carly asked.

Gabriel shook his head in disbelief. "That's a hundred and fifty miles per hour. We've never seen a sailboat travel more than sixty miles per hour on Earth. This ship is awesome."

Dash had been quiet, thinking about everything they'd seen and experienced so far. Now he turned to the captain and said quietly, "Everything is Pollen Slither, isn't it? The clothes you're wearing, that stretchy material that saved us back there, and the sails. It's all Pollen Slither."

The captain nodded. She held out a piece of fabric from her robes and let them touch it. The material felt like running a hand over water.

"This is the treasure of our planet. In its pure form, it resides at the bottom of the sea behind mountains of stone. We are able to capture pure Pollen Slither that leaks from underwater mountains and create the things we need to survive here. It is everything to us. It is why you are in grave danger."

"What do you mean?" Carly asked.

"The pirates came here long ago, like you have come here now. They don't know how to harvest Pollen Slither from our sea, so they take it from us."

The captain touched the fabric on her face and winced.

"What's wrong?" Dash asked.

The captain paused briefly before she began to gently unwrap the cloth from her face.

When her veil was lifted, the Voyagers saw a slightly pink face, like a child who had been in the sun too long. Her lips and large, round eyes were a startling blue.

"Huh, I was picturing a lizard face," Gabriel whispered out of the corner of his mouth. "But this is better!"

"She's amazing," Carly whispered back.

Dash was more concerned with the color of her skin, which had changed since he'd seen her face the first time.

"You're burned," he observed. "Is it because you took off your covering out there?"

The captain removed a small container from somewhere inside the flowing fabric and dabbed her finger into a liquid. She applied it to her pink skin as she spoke.

"The sun here burns hot, and our skin is different than yours. Pollen Slither will help."

She removed a thin blue glove from her hand and reached out toward Carly's face.

"Your hand is cold," Carly said. "Like ice."

"Your face is rough," the captain said gently, touching Carly's cheek. "Like leather."

Gabriel held back a laugh. "Leather face. Nice."

"Exposure to the sun for more than a few minutes can kill the AquaGen. It has always been this way. It's one of the reasons we fear the red pirates. They're not only bigger than us, their armor protects them from weapons we might use against them. If they wanted to rip our veils off, they could—and have. So we give them what they want, again and again."

"I hate bullies," Gabriel grumbled.

The captain sighed sadly. She covered her face once more and put her medicine away.

"I'm a captain too," Dash said. "Carly and Gabriel here, we're all on the same crew. And there's another girl named Piper waiting for us up there, where you can't see her. She's a kid too. These people aren't just my crew; they're my friends. We're Voyagers. We're not here to harm you or take anything from you. We're trying to save our own planet. All we need is a small amount of pure Pollen Slither. That's it. I promise, one captain to another, we'll leave and never come back."

The captain looked at each of them in turn.

"What's your name?" Carly asked as she touched her own cheek, trying to remember what the coolness of the captain's hand had felt like.

"Somselia," the captain said. "I am from a long line of ship's captains. Too long to count."

"It's a beautiful name," Carly said.

Dash stood, holding on to the rail of the bed for balance. "We need your help, Somselia. Will you please help us?"

Somselia looked at her own hands, rubbing them together as if she was trying to create heat. They heard the red pirate outside, its giant feet slamming into the floor as it paced back and forth.

The captain looked at all of them again and spoke: "I don't know what they will do to you when they finish taking what they came for. But if I can help you, I will."

"Are we sure this is a good idea?" Gabriel asked. "We could easily ruin the whole thing and then what will we do?" The Voyagers were still trapped in the belly of an alien ship, bored and more than a little seasick.

"I can rewire it," Carly said. "You know I'm good with electronics. Trust me, this is going to work."

Gabriel held out his hand and asked to see the translator. Carly handed it over reluctantly.

"My mom once took apart a phone and tried to put a new screen on it," Gabriel said. "She was good with electronics too. There were a lot of parts left over when she was done, and we ended up with a really expensive doorstop."

Carly looked at Dash. "It's your call. I'm telling you, Dash. I can do it."

Carly understood the risk of destroying the device, but she also figured they might only have a little more time together where they weren't being watched. They had no other technology to speak of; it had all been taken from them. Their wrist tech had been in Somselia's teardrop-shaped bag, which had been confiscated by the red pirates. They needed to try something.

"If we destroy the translator, then we won't be able

to communicate with Somselia," Gabriel was quick to re-mind them. "Are we really willing to risk cutting our com-munication with everyone on Aqua Gen?"

Dash thought this was a really good point, but he also knew that what Carly was proposing to do might be the only way to save them. He looked at Somselia. "You're a captain too. What do you think?"

Somselia paused a moment before answering. "I don't think these red pirates are going to let you leave here. They don't know who you are or where you came from. I think Carly is right. I don't see any other way."

"Then I think we should do it," Dash said. "It might be our only shot at getting off this planet. What do you think, Gabriel?"

"If I'm the deciding vote, I say no way," Gabriel said. "It's too risky."

"Sitting here doing nothing is what's too risky," Carly shot back. She looked at Dash for support.

"It's three against one," Dash agreed. "We need to trust Carly."

Gabriel took one last look at the prized device. "We never got to use the Darth Vader voice setting. It's a tragedy."

"Darth Vader?" Somselia said curiously. "What is Darth Vader?"

Gabriel cracked a smile and shook his head. "Only the most famous villain in the entire universe!"

Somselia didn't know what to make of this, but there

was no time to explain as Gabriel reluctantly handed over the translator and fell back on the bed. "I don't feel good about this."

"You will," Carly said confidently.

During the next half hour, the ship sailed at 150 miles per hour, taking them to places unknown, as Carly took the translator apart piece by piece. The device was equipped with two small tools that slid into cavities built into the casing. One was a wrench with a tiny six-sided star on the end. The other was a set of tweezers on one end and a sharp point on the other. Somewhere in the middle of the process, Gabriel sat up and looked at the work area on the floor. The translator was in about a hundred pieces.

"I think I'm gonna be sick," he said, and lay back down.

Dash watched as Carly examined each of the intricate parts, turning them in her hands and reordering them on the floor.

"No turning back now," Dash said. "You can do this, Carly."

"I know," Carly said.

And then Carly started cobbling together pieces very quickly. Within a few minutes, there were half as many items to use. She worked with complete poise and focus, like a brilliant kid with a complicated Lego model that needed building.

"There," she said at length. "It's finished."

"I can't look," Gabriel said.

"Don't be alarmed when you see it," Dash said. He'd watched it being built, so the shock wasn't as severe. Still, it was quite a transformation.

"What in the—?" Gabriel said when he saw the device. He looked at Dash. "We're doomed."

"Nope, not doomed," Carly said. "I turned it into a communication device."

All the electronic guts of the translator were strung together in a long, jagged line that reached almost from the floor to the ceiling. A few lights blinked here and there along the tracks of components, and wires hung loose like little rubber chicken heads searching for food.

"This is a disaster," Gabriel said. "We can't communicate with somersault lady anymore."

"Somselia," Carly said with a smile.

"What?" Gabriel shot back.

"That's the captain's name. Somselia."

Gabriel just shook his head. "We're doomed."

Even Dash had to admit he had his doubts, but he wasn't going to say anything. What good would it do? Either the device would work or it wouldn't.

Carly crouched down low next to the base of the contraption and moved a circular dial.

"What are the coordinates we sent Piper to?" Carly asked confidently.

Gabriel called out the coordinates. Carly dialed back and forth like the spin lock on a school locker. When she was done, she held two of the dangling wires together and spoke into the tiny mike, which she had removed from its casing.

"Piper, do you read me? Come in, Piper."

They waited for a few seconds and got no reply, but Carly didn't falter. "Come in, *Cloud Cat*. Do you read me?"

Ten seconds later, still nothing.

"I *know* this is right!" Carly said. She paced back and forth. "Give me the coordinates for the *Cloud Leopard*."

"It's not going to matter," Gabriel said. "You broke it."

Carly put her face right up to Gabriel's. "Give. Me. The. Coordinates."

Gabriel's eyes went wide. He doled out the three numbers that would give Carly the exact location of the *Cloud Leopard*.

Carly went right back to work, feverishly working the dial.

While all of this went on, Somselia sat quietly observing. Now and then she would say something in her gurgle-filled voice, but the Voyagers couldn't understand what she was saying.

"You guys, I think the ship is slowing down," Dash said.

They all felt it. The ship was coming to its destination, wherever that was.

"STEAM 6000, do you read me? Come in, STEAM," Carly said.

Again, dead air. Nothing.

Carly ran her hands over every part of the five-foot-tall mess of wires, circuit boards, and random parts.

"STEAM, please," Carly said on the verge of tears. "Come in."

Dash felt terrible for Carly. "It's okay, Carly. I made the call. This was my mistake."

"It wasn't a mistake!" Carly snapped. She sat down on the bunk next to Gabriel and stared at the crazy device she'd built. It looked like a Rube Goldberg puzzle gone terribly wrong. She covered her face in disappointment. "I want to go home."

"You know what," Dash said as he felt the ship lurch to a stop. "I believe in you. And we're going to get through this. Failure is not an option."

Carly's brow furrowed. "Failure is not an option," she repeated.

"Yeah," Gabriel said, feeling bad for doubting Carly. "What you guys said. We'll figure something out."

Then they heard a familiar tinny voice, far away and small, but very real.

"STEAM 6000, receiving your message," STEAM said. "What do you need?"

Somselia's eyes went wide.

Carly scrambled down onto the floor. With shaking hands, she held the wires together and spoke. "STEAM! Can you hear me?"

"I have already confirmed," STEAM said. "Yes, I can hear you."

Dash and Gabriel got down on their knees on either side of Carly.

"Ask him if he can calculate our location," Dash said frantically.

Carly asked, her voice cracking with excitement.

"Of course I can," STEAM said.

Dash heard heavy footsteps approaching, followed by low red pirate voices outside the door. A second red pirate had made its way down into the hull of the ship.

Carly went on: "STEAM, we need you to track this device location. Call the *Cloud Cat* back to the main ship remotely. Then get down here and retrieve us! But listen, STEAM, be careful. These AquaGens are touchy about visitors. Got it?"

"I understand completely, yes sir!" STEAM said. "Initiating Mother Hen directive pronto."

"Weird robot," Gabriel said.

The voices outside the door sounded like they were arguing, but no one could be sure.

"Which part is the GPS?" Dash asked.

Carly reached into the glob of technology with the star screwdriver. In seconds, she had removed a component no bigger than her thumbnail.

"This is it," Carly said. "But you'll need some power."

She dug back in while Dash and Gabriel looked on in wonder.

"You really are a master tech-tinkering genius," Gabriel said.

Carly didn't look up when she answered. "I know."

She pulled out a red wire attached to something that

looked like a magnet. It was about the size of a quarter. Dash held the GPS out toward her, and she attached the wire.

"There," she said. "That should stay charged for long enough. And STEAM can track it wherever we go."

"You are awesome, Carly!" Dash said.

"Never doubted you for a minute," Gabriel added. Dash leveled him with a stare cold enough to freeze a Wookiee, and Gabriel smiled.

Carly nodded appreciatively, but it only lasted a fraction of a second. The boat tilted hard to one side, sending all three of them diving for the bunk beds.

"What's going on out there?" Carly asked.

The latch on the door was moving. Someone was coming in.

"I think we're about to find out," Gabriel said.

Dash looked at Somselia and hoped she understood. "We're going to be okay. You'll see."

As the door opened and two giant red pirates strode in, something was rattling inside Dash's head that wouldn't stop bothering him. The communication device had worked. They'd been able to reach STEAM on the *Cloud Leopard* just fine, and it was farther away than the *Cloud Cat*.

So where was Piper?

The bridge of the *Cloud Cat* was empty. Other than a few beeps and the swishing of the wind battering the exterior, there were no sounds at all. No Rocket, no Piper. The ship was not stationed high overhead, hidden from the view of Aqua Gen as the rest of the crew thought. Piper had moved it much closer to the surface. In fact, the *Cloud Cat* was hovering only twenty feet off the water, holding its position above a very specific location.

Farther back in the small ship, where the bay doors had opened and deployed the crew a day earlier, Piper's air chair was floating around in a circle.

The air chair was empty.

And the sleek two-man submarine that could travel twenty thousand feet under the sea of an alien planet was gone.

The ship rocked hard again in the direction of the door, and all three Voyagers tumbled out of the bunk. They hit the floor and crashed right over the cobbled together communication tower, breaking it into pieces.

One of the red pirates tried to push its way through the door, but it was too wide. Instead it swung one arm, putting a metal-clad fist through the wall like it was made of paper. A few more swings and the red pirate had opened a big enough space to walk into the room. It crouched down and examined the broken mechanical parts on the floor, then stared bullets at Somselia. The red pirate howled loudly and put a finger right up in Somselia's face.

"I think it's a little upset," Gabriel said. "Maybe it thinks we made a communication device so we can try to escape."

"That's exactly what we did!" Carly said.

"Guys, stay calm," Dash advised. "Freaking out isn't going to do us any good against these guys."

Somselia put her hands up and seemed to be trying to calm the red pirate down, but it wasn't doing any good. It pushed her forward, out of the room and into the hall. The red pirate motioned for the Voyagers to do the same.

"I hope STEAM knows what he's doing," Gabriel said as they filed out of the room.

All the AquaGens were pouring out of the holding cells, ushered back to the upper deck by colossal red pirates. As one of the AquaGens passed Somselia, Dash noticed that he discreetly handed her something. But what was it?

The AquaGens moved like liquid, sliding their bodies back and forth as if they were made of water as the ship rocked wildly. When Dash looked up, they were talking in their gargle-and-squeak voices again.

"This isn't feeling right," Dash said to his crew. "We should be prepared to make a run for it."

"Dash, I hate to break this to you, but we're on a boat," Carly said. "There's no place to run."

Dash filed in right behind Somselia. He could hear her trying to communicate with him in a garbled whisper.

"I can't understand you," he whispered, shaking his head and pointing to his ear. He wished there had been a way to communicate with STEAM *and* keep the translator in one piece, but they couldn't have had both.

As they walked up the steep set of wooden stairs, the ship rocked them hard into the narrow walls. Dash felt something pressed into his hand and looked back again at Somselia. It was dark in the rising passage of stairs and he couldn't see what it was, but he held on to it until the door was flung open above and light poured in.

As soon as he saw what Somselia had given him, Dash tapped Carly on the shoulder and handed her two of the three MTBs. She handed one to Gabriel, and in seconds, they had all slid them back on their forearms like fingerless gloves. And just like that, they were back in business!

Suddenly, Somselia was yelling something at the red

pirates. They argued back and forth as water began to flow down the stairs and rain pelted the Voyagers from the opening.

"This is some storm," Carly said.

"Yeah," Gabriel agreed.

Dash was only half listening. From his location farther down on the stairs, he could see enough to work the pad on his wrist tech. He was feverishly typing, sending an all-important message to STEAM.

I need translator software now!

Dash pushed Gabriel and Carly in front of him so he'd have a little more time. The captain pulled Gabriel through the door, and he disappeared into the haze of the storm. Carly next. Dash was just a few steps down into the hull. He only had one chance. A few seconds and it would be gone.

Come on, STEAM!

The MTBs weren't equipped to do high-end translating, but STEAM was. If he could keep STEAM on the line . . .

"There! I have it," Dash said. He tapped out a rapid-fire command and turned to Somselia. "I can understand you again. What's happening?"

STEAM was listening in, prepared to translate both sides of the conversation. Dash held his wrist next to Somselia's hidden face and pointed to where she needed to speak.

She spoke, and a few seconds later, STEAM translated.

"The red pirates are throwing you off the ship," STEAM said. "She thought she could convince them to change their minds, but she could not. She is sorry."

What? Dash thought. But this was no time to panic. His mind went into high gear. He believed Somselia was his ally and he'd have to trust that feeling. He didn't have much else he could hold on to.

Except, maybe . . .

"STEAM," Dash said quickly. "Can you upload the translator software to my MTB?"

"Yes sir," STEAM said. His voice was small and far away in the MTB speaker. "AquaGen translation module created, tested, and deployed."

"Great, thanks," Dash replied. "Stand by. I think I have an idea. . . ."

Step one complete. Now Dash could communicate with Somselia on his own again. Time for step two. Dash contacted STEAM once more and gave the robot an order he told no one else about.

When he reached the deck of the ship, it was total chaos. The Pollen Slither sails had been taken down as the storm whipped water five feet over the bow. The AquaGens took it in stride, as if storms such as these were a common occurrence they simply had to outlast. When waves of water hit them, they simply stood their ground. They seemed to become part of the water itself, merging and melting into it, and then reappearing on the other side.

The red pirates were stationed all around the deck, and the waves didn't do anything to even budge them off their feet. They must have weighed five hundred pounds each with all that armor.

"Dash!" Gabriel yelled. "Over here!"

Gabriel and Carly were standing on the far edge of the ship at the bottom of a ladder leading up. The ladder ended at a small platform with a pole sticking up the middle. It appeared to be attached to a plank that could be pushed out over the surface of the water. Dash ran to his friends. Lashed by sideways rain and whipping wind, he was knocked off his feet and rolled down the deck. Two red pirates picked him up, one at each arm, and hauled him to where Gabriel and Carly were standing.

"What are we going to do?" Gabriel asked, water running down his face in tracks as he threw his hand through his wet hair. He looked pleadingly at Dash, his friend and his captain.

A group of pirates, all in red metal armor and mirrored-glass helmets, surrounded the Alpha team. They pointed to the ladder leading to the platform as a wall of water rose up and crashed over the bow, slamming down on the ship. The Voyagers held on to the ladder for dear life, and when they looked up, Somselia was standing next to them.

"Please," she called out to the pirates.

Dash grabbed the AquaGen captain's arm. "Tell these bullies to leave and never attack another AquaGen ship again! Tell them that you have terrible and powerful allies!" he pleaded. "Tell them they'll be sorry!"

Somselia looked confused, but she turned to the group of red pirates and delivered Dash's message nevertheless. All three of the red pirates standing there began to shake and howl. Then they turned and bellowed something to the rest of the pirates, and they were all shaking and howling.

"I think they're laughing at you, bro," Gabriel said. "Bummer."

But Dash didn't mind. He looked at his best friend. "They won't be laughing for long."

The red pirates stopped roaring and pushed Dash, Carly, and Gabriel up the ladder. To their surprise, Somselia followed them onto the platform.

As soon as all four of them were on the round platform, it began to move out over the water. They held on to the pole for dear life as they were transported away from the ship by a plank that extended ten feet.

Out over the water, the storm was a swirling, raging monster. Water twisted and rose up in ways the Voyagers had never seen before. It was beyond wild, like they were trapped inside a blender set to churn a chocolate milk shake.

"Dash!" Gabriel yelled. "I have bad news!"

"I know, Gabriel," Dash said. "We're all gonna die. Not the best time for a joke buddy."

"No! I mean it!" Gabriel said. He was pointing out

into the haze of the storm as lightning flashed and thunder roared across the face of the ship.

It was difficult to see at first, a smear of darkness moving toward them, but in the lightning crash, Dash saw it too: a sleek ship, modern and curved, with rows of teeth painted across its front. "The enemy approaches!" Dash's MTB translated. "They have come to retrieve their shipmates. And their Pollen Slither."

"Zombie pirates!" Gabriel shouted into the wind. "This is now officially the worst and most awesome thing ever!"

Dash watched as the pirate vessel came closer, the painted teeth each as tall as he was. They looked like a mouth ready to eat the ship whole. Or slam into it.

"It's going to hit us!" Dash yelled.

Dash had his arm wrapped around the pole at the elbow, feverishly working on his wrist tech. He looked at Somselia, touching her on the arm to get her attention.

"I know the universe seems like a bad place," Dash said. "But we're not like them. Let me help you."

After a moment, Somselia nodded slowly. "If you can help, the time is now."

Dash tapped a final command into his wrist tech and spoke.

"STEAM?"

"I'm almost there, sir," STEAM answered. Normally the *Cloud Leopard* would be a full fifteen minutes from the surface of Aqua Gen, but STEAM was pushing the ship much faster than an everyday rendezvous. The ship had gone the distance in half that.

"Hurry!" Dash yelled.

And then he saw it. The *Cloud Leopard.* Dash had completely forgotten what a colossus the *Cloud Leopard* was from the outside. And the way STEAM came in— hotter than hot—their ship blew everyone's mind right out of the water. It nosed down from the sky, breaking through the clouds and cutting sharply. A black shadow descended over the AquaGen ship as the *Cloud Leopard* slowed to a complete stop. Overhead, the hull of the ship was like a football field of mechanical awesomeness, miles of metal built into one gargantuan machine.

"If I didn't know better," Gabriel said, "I'd be scared out of my pants right now."

"Move in slow," Dash said into his wrist tech. "Let them know what they're dealing with."

The ship's nose tilted downward, and the *Cloud Leopard* inched forward. Dash could feel the power of the motors in the bottom of his gut. Like a thundering backbeat on the loudest bass ever played, it shook the teeth inside his head.

The rain was blocked overhead, so they could watch everything clearly from their perch on the small platform. STEAM brought the ship closer, directly over the pirate vessel.

As the *Cloud Leopard* descended, it quickly became clear that it was at least thirty times the size of the pirate ship. The red pirates on the AquaGen ship weren't quite so emboldened as they had been. A few of them jumped into the sea and began swimming for their own ship. Some stood their ground, staring up at the *Cloud Leopard.*

"Twelve seconds to impact," STEAM said.

"Hold," Dash ordered. He looked at Somselia. "What do you want me to do?"

Somselia gazed at the pirate ship and Dash wondered about all that she'd been through. How many pirate ships had been used as torpedoes to cut through AquaGen ships like balsa wood? How much of their Pollen Slither had been stolen? How many of her sailors had she lost? It would be understandable if she'd asked Dash to lower the boom on her greedy enemy, but that wasn't technically an option.

"We don't carry large-scale weapons on our ship," Dash said to Somselia. "Its bark is bigger than its bite."

Somselia turned to Dash, and her eyes narrowed as if she was smiling beneath the veil.

"They don't know that," she said. "And they never will. Can you go a little lower?"

"Dash," Gabriel jumped in. "Tell STEAM to initiate Operation Pancake."

"Initiate Operation Pancake?" Dash repeated.

"Pardon me, sir," STEAM responded. "I'm not aware of a pancake operation."

Gabriel rolled his eyes and spoke into Dash's MTB.

"Take it in closer. As close as you can. We need to scare these red pirates good."

"Understood," STEAM said. "Initiating Operation Pancake."

Gabriel smiled and glanced at Dash. "I love getting STEAM to say goofy stuff."

The *Cloud Leopard* lowered even more, until it was nearly parked on top of the pirate ship. Its great turbine engines roared and sent waves of water across the sea. Dash could feel the sound vibrating all the way down his spine and into his legs.

The last of the red pirates dove overboard and swam for their own ship, leaving behind the sails they'd come to steal.

"Their ship has stopped advancing," Somselia said. And then, with marked astonishment in her alien voice, she leaned forward with wide eyes and said something more. "They're *retreating.*"

When everyone looked back, Dash included, the pirate ship was indeed moving away from the AquaGen ship, but not in the way Dash expected it to. The ship seemed to vanish before their eyes. The water enveloped it on every side, and suddenly the pirate ship was simply gone. All that remained was the bubbling surface of the AquaGen ocean.

"No way!" Gabriel said. "We're not dealing with zombie pirates. They're *ghost* pirates!"

"That's no ghost ship," Carly said. "It's a submarine."

"Oh, right," Gabriel said bashfully. "Cool sub."

Dash finally understood why the AquaGens feared the red pirates so much.

"They arrive without any warning and take your treasured sails," Dash said to Somselia. She nodded.

"What an unfair advantage," Carly observed. "It's terrible."

As the Voyagers and the AquaGen captain were helped off the platform and back onto the ship, a call came in from STEAM requesting orders. He still held the *Cloud Leopard* low over the water.

Dash turned to Somselia. "How fast can you get this ship out of here?"

Somselia called to the AquaGens standing nearby on the deck, then returned her gaze to Dash.

"We can't move until the storm passes. It's too dangerous."

The sea was still churning with waves as the wind lashed the side of the ship and dark gray clouds churned overhead.

As a hard rain continued to fall, Gabriel looked skyward and got an idea. He tapped into his communication with the ship. "STEAM? Listen, can you get right over the top of us again? Tilt your nose toward the water and cut some of this wind off the ship. Stay overhead when we move. Got it? Operation . . . uh, Windshield."

"Directive received," STEAM said. "Complying."

The *Cloud Leopard* rose frighteningly fast, leveling

out and turning toward the AquaGen vessel. Somselia told her frightened crew to stay calm as the *Cloud Leopard* moved back above the AquaGen ship, dipped its nose, and began to move slowly. The terrified crew understood it was an escape option and flew into action, hoisting countless sails overhead. The massive hull of the *Cloud Leopard* cut about half the wind and protected them all from the pelting rain.

"Operation Windshield under way, yes sir!" STEAM said once it appeared the plan was going to work.

"STEAM is awesome!" Gabriel said. "I'm so hanging out with our robot buddy when we get back. I gotta hear the blow-by-blow from the deck firsthand."

Dash was all business, watching the water for any sign of a returning pirate sub. "How many pirate subs are there?" he asked Somselia.

The commander took a moment to ponder and then shrugged. "A hundred?"

Dash imagined a hundred submarines, trolling the seas of Aqua Gen, searching for ships to destroy. He shuddered at the thought.

"But I don't think they'll be bothering us anymore," Somselia said. "I think you've made them think twice about the friends we have in high places."

Dash couldn't see her face, but he was sure she was smiling.

"How long have they been here?" Dash asked.

"Since before I was born," Somselia said. "But we

rarely lose ships anymore. We're good at keeping away from them. It will be much easier now."

Dash lifted his arm to speak into his MTB. "What's the status of the pirate sub?" he asked STEAM.

"It's big enough to keep on radar up to seven thousand feet," STEAM said. "It moved off about three hundred yards and dove. I lost its location approximately ten seconds ago."

Dash finally relaxed. He shared the good news with Somselia, who turned to the entire crew and spoke at the top of her lungs. "We're safe. This group of visitors has saved us today. They are our friends."

Then Somselia raised her hands to the crown of her head and removed the silver band. It was solid, like a magician's ring of steel. She splayed her thumbs and forefingers along the edges of the ring and began to rock her hands back and forth in the movement of a wave.

"This, too, is Pollen Slither," she told Dash. "It takes many forms and has many uses. In this form, after heating over a fire, it can be resized."

The ring became smaller and smaller, until it was only the diameter of a coffee cup. And smaller still, until she had forged a ring of silver before their eyes. She held it out to Dash.

"I can't take your captain's ring," Dash said.

Somselia took Dash's hand and turned it up, placing the treasure in his palm.

"I know a good captain when I see one," she said, closing his fingers around the ring. "Besides, I can make another one. We have plenty of Pollen Slither on Aqua Gen. Consider this a gift for helping us."

"Wow, dude," Gabriel said. "I think you just got married."

Carly laughed so hard she snorted.

But Dash knew better. One captain to another, this was the most important thing she could have given him. He slipped the ring on his finger and felt a sense of pride.

Somselia gazed skyward, where the sky was blotted out by the great shadow of the *Cloud Leopard.* Then she turned to everyone on the ship and made a weird, watery sound that didn't translate. It must have been a rare command that wasn't recognized by the translation software. Everyone in the crew stopped what they were doing and looked at Dash, Carly, and Gabriel. And then they bowed, smiled, and turned to the sea all at once.

Carly looked to the water too. "Why are they all staring out into the storm?"

The captain took a deep breath of the sea air. "We have had many bad things happen to us on this water, but today is a victory. It is what we call a miracle."

"Oh sure, we know about miracles," Gabriel said. "I once saw Winnie-the-Pooh's head staring back at me on the surface of a waffle. True story."

Dash didn't bother translating Gabriel's "miracle," but he did laugh.

"Gabriel, you rock my world," Dash said.

"Mine too," Carly said.

Not long after that, with the AquaGen ship safely out of harm's way, three hoisting cables were released from the belly of the *Cloud Leopard*. They danced in the wind until the Voyagers crew put the harnesses on and stood at the ready.

"Will we ever see you again?" Somselia asked as she looked up at the ship with wonder in her eyes.

"I hope so," Dash said. "Would you welcome us?"

She touched him on the shoulder. It felt like a cold, liquid hand. "You are always welcome here. You and your crew will be remembered."

Dash was feeling close to amazing as they rose up into the *Cloud Leopard*.

By the time the *Cloud Leopard* broke through the storm and arrived on the other side of the clouds, they remembered that Piper had been strangely silent. Where was she? Gabriel took control of the ship as STEAM tried to get Dash's attention.

"Can I see you privately, Captain?" STEAM asked.

Dash didn't respond as he watched the dark clouds swirl below the ship.

"I've locked onto the *Cloud Cat,*" Gabriel said. "We can rendezvous in approximately seven minutes."

"I'm not getting any response," Carly reported. "Where could she be?"

"Sir, a word, please," STEAM said again, nudging Dash with a mechanical arm.

"What's the problem, STEAM?" Dash asked, distracted. But STEAM didn't answer. Instead, the robot moved quickly toward the boys' quarters and Dash followed.

When they arrived at Dash's bedside, Dash suddenly remembered.

"Oh, right, my daily injection," Dash said, embarrassed that he'd forgotten something so important. "I've had a lot on my mind."

"I understand," STEAM replied. "You are very much behind schedule. Please administer the shot immediately."

"Thanks, STEAM," Dash said. He carefully set up the device and placed it against his arm. The shots didn't hurt, but they did feel strange and Dash always cringed. He still hadn't gotten used to giving himself injections. Or keeping the information from his friends.

"You may return to active duty, sir," STEAM said. "But I am going to reprogram your MTB with a reminder alarm so that this delay does not happen again."

Dash was about to leave, but he hesitated at the door and turned back.

"Why do you think Piper isn't answering?" he asked.

STEAM made some whirling sounds, as if it was taking a moment to calculate its answer.

"There are three possible scenarios," the robot said. "She has fallen asleep, she has left the ship, or she is—"

"Don't say it," Dash said abruptly, cutting STEAM off. "Option three is not an option."

He knew what option three was, how could he not? But there was no way things had gotten that bad, right?

Dash looked at his MTB. "We'll be able to board in a couple of minutes. You take the *Cloud Leopard* back into orbit, we'll take it from here."

"As you wish," STEAM said.

When Dash arrived back on the main deck, Gabriel was already manually docking the *Cloud Cat* in the hangar.

"The ship is yours," Gabriel said, relinquishing command to STEAM.

A few minutes later, Dash, Carly, and Gabriel arrived in the docking bay, where the *Cloud Cat* was waiting for them.

"It doesn't look damaged in any way," Carly said, walking around the side and searching for problems. "It appears to be in good shape."

Dash pressed a series of commands on his MTB, and the door hissed open on hydraulic arms. It was a strange moment: they all wanted to go inside right away, but then again they sort of didn't.

"What if we find bad news in there?" Carly asked.

"That's not going to happen," Dash said. "There has to be a logical explanation for why Piper hasn't contacted us."

"Only one way to find out," Gabriel said, and taking a deep breath, he started up the ramp. Dash and Carly followed. Once inside, they spread out looking for Piper.

They didn't need to look very far to discover the missing submarine.

"She's gone," Dash concluded.

"Looks like she took Rocket," Gabriel said. "First dog to travel twenty thousand feet under the sea of an alien planet. I bet that will make headlines back home."

"But why would she do this on her own?" Dash asked.

"She must have thought we might not come back," Carly said. She looked back and forth between Dash and

Gabriel. "We were offline for a long time. The location of the Pollen Slither must have calculated a while ago. She probably tried to reach us and then finally gave up."

Dash didn't know what to say. He slumped down in one of the navigation chairs and tried to think. They had no Pollen Slither, and Piper had vanished into the deepest part of an alien sea.

But that didn't mean they were out of the game. Not yet. Dash had an idea.

"How fast can you get this thing back down to the surface?" Dash asked.

Gabriel just smiled, locked into his seat, and started the engines.

Ship's log 12.12

[Alpha team member: Dash Conroy]

[Comm link: audio feed, *Cloud Cat*]

> *This is Dash Conroy, leader of the Voyagers Alpha team. Everything that could have gone wrong did go wrong. We're lucky to be alive.*

[A seven-second break in the message occurs here.]

> *We are currently missing one member of our team. The situation on the surface is too unstable for reentry. I'm on the deck of the Cloud Cat, staring down at a tornado churning the watery surface of Aqua Gen.*

[A four-second break in the message occurs here.]

If I can't bring our teammate back, I will resign my post effective immediately.

[End of transmission]

2 Hours Earlier.

"I really, truly, totally cannot believe I'm doing this," Piper said.

Rocket barked once, which she took as the dog's agreement that they were in over their heads. Literally. He sat in the front seat, which had a lower viewpoint out into the sea than the backseat. Piper reached up and scratched behind Rocket's ear, where he liked it best.

If not for Rocket, Piper didn't think she would have the courage to even sit down inside the sub, let alone launch it into the sea. She hovered next to the watercraft, staring at the two seats while her heart pounded and her hands shook. The *V* for *Voyagers* blazed across the side of the otherwise sky-blue submarine. No glass dome covered the cockpit, just open air, and Rocket had leapt into the front seat.

"I see what you're doing," Piper said. "I'm not getting in."

Rocket whimpered and set his sad face on the edge of the submarine.

Piper had tried the extraction crew over and over, waiting for a response that was not going to come. The future of the entire world rested on making sure they retrieved all six elements and created the Source. And without Pollen Slither, there would be no going back home. What if she was their only hope of retrieving it?

"You're not getting out, are you?" Piper asked. Rocket barked but remained in the seat.

Piper took a deep breath. Then another. She drove in a circle around the whole sub, checking it for problems like she was about to buy a used car. Everything looked perfectly fine.

"I can do this," Piper said.

But saying you could do something and actually doing it was like standing on the edge of a bridge attached to a bungee cord. There was a lot of talk of jumping and very little actual jumping. Until finally you really did jump, which is exactly what Piper did. Without even knowing how she'd gotten there, she found herself sitting in the Alpha sub, setting the various controls she'd learned in training.

"I hope Chris was right about this cover," Piper said, pressing an egg-shaped icon on the screen in front of her. It went from red to green as a clear dome rose up around her. It covered the whole cab of the Alpha sub like honey spilling over the back of a spoon. But unlike honey, this dome was crystal clear and, apparently, as hard as iron. It was a substance Chris had invented called Energy Glass. It protected them from the pressure the depth of the sea created. They could travel deeper and faster than they could under normal circumstances. And when the time came, they could launch to the surface quickly, without the risk of pressure sickness.

She opened the bay doors and looked down at the angry clouds below. She saw lightning flashes inside the clouds and worried even more.

She remembered covering this potential situation in training on the *Cloud Leopard.* It had involved a virtual simulation with a far longer descent through the sky. The solution was already programmed into the sub. There was an icon for it: a parachute.

Piper's finger stayed poised over that button for a long time before she finally gave in.

She jumped.

She pressed the button.

The bay doors opened, and the Alpha sub launched into the open air. It felt like Piper had just reached the top of a roller coaster, plummeting back to Earth on the other side. The storm lashed the Alpha sub through the clouds and the open air beneath, turning it like a corkscrew as the sea rose up on every side.

"This was a bad idea!" Piper screamed. "A really, really bad idea!"

Rocket barked happily.

The sub plunged into the sea, rocketing straight down into the depths. Piper gazed out into clear water as the sub slowed. When she'd reached five thousand feet below the surface, her MTB lost its connection to the outside world. Darkness lay at the edges all around her.

The Alpha sub was equipped with a powerful headlight. Piper turned it on, and as the light illuminated the black water, she saw the many creatures of Aqua Gen for the first time. There were strange fish in bright colors, swimming in schools far too big to count. They rolled over the sub, parting and reforming, moving along the deep currents of open space.

"Rocket, look there," Piper said, pointing over the dog's left shoulder. Rocket's head turned in that direction, and through the distant light, a wall of alien-like creatures, thousands deep, moved quietly across their view. They looked alarmingly like sharks, and Piper had always feared sharks in particular. She felt a thunder of dread roll through her body as they passed through the wall of teeth and fins. The Alpha sub bumped back and forth, cutting a path. One of the creatures opened its mouth and tried to bite into the sub, knocking it sideways as teeth slammed down.

"This is the worst day of my life," Piper said, her eyes clenched shut as the sub spun back on course. When she opened them again, they had cleared the way, going deeper still.

Piper gathered her nerves and checked the map. They were fifteen thousand feet below now, and looking up, she saw something that took her breath away. It was like

the northern lights underwater, a shimmering wave of every color rising like a ribbon through the sea.

"It's Pollen Slither," Piper said, an unexpected smile on her face. "We must be getting close to the source."

A much bigger fish, the size of a school bus, moved slowly past in the distance. It was opening its mouth, eating something that glowed with a soft neon light.

"They're like jellyfish," Piper said as they came upon a group of the same creatures. They moved in slow motion, their translucent bodies filling and emptying with water. Each one radiated soft purple-and-blue light, moving silently as if they didn't have a care in the world. Rocket barked, and Piper refocused on the giant fish in the distant light. Something bigger still loomed out of the darkness, quick and efficient, slamming its teeth down hard. It shook the great fish back and forth as the Alpha sub came closer and Piper named it for what it was.

"Predator Z," she whispered.

The beast looked directly at the Alpha sub with angry eyes. It didn't let go of its prey as the sub came closer.

Piper instinctively killed the headlight. But the purple-and-blue glow from the jellyfish-like creatures radiated into the blackness of the sea and she could see the outline of the great predator as it demolished its prey. Gabriel had programmed the sub to avoid things that were really big. It knew its destination and plotted a new course around the Predator Z, silently slipping by through safer waters.

Piper kept an eye on the massive creature on the radar, and when they were safely past, she reached her hand out toward the touch screen. But she didn't turn the light back on. Not yet. In the distance, she could see another light, its beam cutting across the water like a V turned on its side.

"What kind of creature is this one?" Piper asked out loud. Whatever it was, it hadn't been covered in training. Nothing they studied had the power to cast such a bright light this far underwater. She crept closer, hoping the Predator Z had moved on in search of food somewhere else in the deep sea.

"What do you think it is, Rocket?" Piper asked.

Rocket whimpered curiously, and Piper reached forward and scratched behind his ear. She checked the mapping system and saw how close they were to their destination, where she should be able to find pure Pollen Slither. And that's when it hit her. She was looking at a side view of another submarine with its light on.

She had come upon the Omega crew.

Anna and her team had beaten Piper to the element, but she didn't care. Piper had never been so happy in her whole life. She didn't mind that they were the competition, because she was no longer alone in one of the loneliest places in the universe.

The Omega submarine wasn't moving. The farthest edge of its beam of light was pointed at a wall of jagged rocks. A long tube was attached to the sub, extending out into the water like a tentacle, its far end stuck in a crevice of the rocks.

"They're already extracting Pollen Slither," Piper realized.

Piper activated her MTB and let it search for their frequency. She couldn't reach the surface from fifteen thousand feet underwater, but she should be able to connect with the Omega crew a hundred yards away.

"Omega, do you read me?" Piper said. "Are you there?"

There was a moment of silence that seemed to last forever, but then Piper heard a voice she knew all too well.

"Well, if it isn't the Alpha team," Anna Turner said. "We were wondering when you might show up."

"I'm so glad you're down here with me!" Piper said. She laughed she was so happy. "It's pretty crazy, right?"

"Sure, I guess," Anna said.

"Anna," Ravi said.

"Hey, Ravi!" Piper said happily.

"There's something approaching," Ravi said. "It's big."

"I just passed a Predator Z," Piper said with alarm. "This isn't good."

"Why didn't you say so?" Anna asked.

"Ravi, turn your light off!" Piper instructed.

"Don't tell my navigation officer what to do," Anna shot back.

"It's not a sea creature," Ravi said, concern growing in his voice. "It's something else."

The Omega sub's V-shaped beam of light grew larger

as it went farther out into the water. At the end of the light, the front of the biggest fish Piper had ever seen appeared. It was lined with an open mouth full of teeth.

"Let's get out of here!" Piper yelled.

But the Omega ship didn't move.

"The extraction is almost complete," Anna said. "Don't cut it yet."

Piper couldn't believe Anna's resolve to get an element for the Source.

"It's not worth the risk, Anna!" Piper said. "Just go!"

Piper looked closer as the fish came into view, and she began to realize something.

This wasn't a fish at all.

It was a submarine.

The pirates of Aqua Gen had found them.

13

"We have it!" Anna yelled. "Go! Go! Go!"

The tube came free from the rocks, leaving a trail of pure Pollen Slither, twisting and turning in the water. The neon blue lava slowly leaked out of the crevice where the tube had been connected.

The pirate ship was bearing down on Omega's tiny sub, pushing it closer to a wall of stone. Piper hadn't realized it before, but she saw now that they'd reached the bottom of the sea. The pirate ship was forcing them into a row of sharp rocks.

Piper turned on her headlight.

"Turn your light off!" she yelled. "I'll distract them!"

The Omega sub's light cut out, and when it was gone, Piper shot straight toward the pirate's sub. She swooped in as close as she dared, arcing up at the last second.

That should get their attention, she thought.

And it did. But the pirate ship was much faster than

Piper thought possible. The sub turned to follow her almost immediately and headed straight for her.

"We're heading to the surface," Anna radioed. "You should do the same. These AquaGens are making me nervous."

"These aren't AquaGens!" Piper said, frantic.

"Whatever they are, get out," Anna said. "We have the element. Move!"

"I'm right behind you," Piper replied, but she couldn't see the Omega sub anywhere as she raced to escape the pirates. The pirate sub had lights of its own. Piper looked back and saw that it was bearing on her fast. The rows of teeth lit up in white, and two more thin beams of light shot toward her.

"I can't outrun it!" Piper shouted.

She took one more look back and braced herself. "Hold on, Rocket!"

The pirate sub slammed into her from behind, sending her end over end through the open water. When she recovered control, she had no idea which way was up or down.

"Get out of there, Piper!" Ravi said.

"I'm hit!" Piper yelled.

"We're coming back for you!" Ravi answered.

"No, it's okay," Piper said. "This is about saving the whole world, not one person. Get that Pollen Slither to the surface before it's too late!"

The Alpha team only had one sub that could do this, and there was a good chance Piper's had just been damaged. It was safe to assume Omega only had one too. If they both failed, the whole mission would fail.

"You have to go," Piper said. "That cargo you're carrying is the most important thing in the universe right now. I'm okay—I'm right behind you. . . ."

But Piper felt the pirate ship slam into her again, this time from above. She heard the gut-wrenching sound of her headlight smashing into pieces.

Piper turned the Alpha sub and headed straight for the rocks where the Omega team had retrieved the Pollen Slither. She sped as fast as the sub would carry her, but the pirate ship was much faster. It crashed again and again into the back of her sub, sending her sideways and upside down as she approached the lowest point on Aqua Gen. When they were but a hundred feet from impact, the pirate ship veered up sharply.

But Piper was tumbling end over end, out of control and heading for the jagged edges of stone in her path. Alarms sounded, lights flashed, and Piper could no longer control the sub.

"This isn't looking good, Rocket!" Piper yelled.

The ship's audio alert system came on.

"Prepare for impact in three, two, one—"

The Alpha sub smashed into rocks, and steam began pouring into the cockpit. The flashing lights stopped, and

the control pad shut down. The sub rolled down the side of the rock wall and rested on the bottom of the sea.

Piper checked herself over—nothing broken, just some bumps and bruises—and then looked out around her. The pirate ship was gone and so were the Omegas.

"Rocket, you okay, boy?" Piper asked.

Rocket whimpered and turned to her. He'd finally had enough adventure for one day.

The systems slowly came back online, though only partly, and Piper did an oxygen check.

She wanted to take a deep breath, to feel her lungs fill. But she didn't. Every breath counted when you only had oxygen for a kid and a dog to last an hour.

Piper unclipped from her seat and leaned forward, doing the same for Rocket. He leapt over the seat and landed in the small space next to Piper's chair. He laid his head on her lap.

"It's okay, Rocket. We're going to figure this out. I promise."

"I'm getting a signal," Gabriel said excitedly. "It's coming in fast, about four thousand feet underwater."

"It's got to be Piper!" Carly said as she turned her chair and looked out the window of the *Cloud Cat.*

"I'll send out a signal and see if I can make contact," Dash said. He approached a communication console. "*Cloud Cat* to Piper, do you read me?"

There was no answer, so Dash changed frequencies and tried again. "Piper, do you read me?"

Another pause, and then a voice filled the *Cloud Cat.* It was not the voice they were hoping to hear.

"You've reached the Omega team," Anna Turner said. "We're coming up now."

"Ask them if they saw Piper," Gabriel said.

"We can't reach Piper," Dash said. "We're pretty sure she's below five thousand feet, so she's out of range. Did you see her down there? Is she with you?"

"She's not with us," Anna said. "But we did encounter the Alpha sub at the extraction point."

This seemed like good news. "So she's doing the extraction and coming up after you?"

Silence. Anna didn't respond.

"Anna?" Dash said. "Is she okay?"

Anna finally returned, her voice as defensive as ever.

"She was when we left, but we ran into some complications. We couldn't stay down there any longer."

Ravi broke in: "Piper saved our bacon, big-time. And that's the truth."

"What happened?" Gabriel asked. He stood up like he was ready to fight. "You better not have left Piper down there in trouble or there's going to *be* some trouble."

"She's the one who told us to leave," Anna said. "Ravi's right. We encountered some kind of submarine down there, a big one. And it was not happy about seeing us in its territory."

"Pirates," Dash spat. "You left Piper down there with *pirates*?"

"It was her call, Dash," Anna said. "She knew the same thing I do: the element is what matters most. Without it, the Earth is doomed and we never get home. It's a good thing we got there first."

"You better keep your distance, Captain Jerk Face!" Gabriel yelled.

But Dash looked thoughtful. "No, maybe she's right, you guys," he said. He pulled the silver ring out of his pocket and looked at it. A good captain did what they had to do. They saw the bigger picture. "Maybe Piper was right too. She understands this mission is bigger than we are. The entire human race is at stake."

"What was going on when you left, Anna?" Carly asked. "Why didn't she follow you out?"

"She started to," Ravi broke in. "But then I think she stayed down there. Maybe she's doing her own extraction now. Either that or she's hiding."

Dash shook his head. He wasn't going to assume Piper was safe. "I need a favor from you, Anna," he said. "Will you let us take your sub back out? We need to go after our teammate."

Anna didn't answer for a long time.

"I would if I could," she finally said, and she sounded sincere. "But it needs recharging or it would never make the whole trip down and back. That takes a minimum of two hours."

"She's right," Ravi said. "How long has Piper been down there?"

Dash checked his MTB.

"Well, we got back to our ship fifty-six minutes ago. But we haven't been able to reach her for longer than that."

"Then I'd guess she's probably got less than an hour of oxygen left," Anna said. "Sorry, Dash. I really am."

"Yeah right!" Gabriel shot back. "If you hadn't done that crazy stunt yesterday that got us all captured we wouldn't be in this mess. If Piper dies, it's on you, Anna Turner."

"Uh, you guys," Carly said.

"This is awful," Ravi said. "There has to be something we can do. Maybe we should go back down quickly—"

"There's not enough of a charge in our sub," Anna snapped. "You know that, Ravi. We'd never make it back."

"You guys?" Carly said again.

"We're about to crest the surface," Ravi said, barely above a whisper. "There's gotta be a way. . . ."

"You guys!" Carly shouted.

Dash and Gabriel turned to Carly and everyone on the Omega team stayed quiet.

"I'm getting a signal from Piper's GPS," Carly said.

She looked at Dash.

"She's on the move."

"**Piper, come in,** Piper!" Gabriel said frantically.

"She's still moving, well within communication range now," Carly said. "About three thousand feet below the surface."

"*Cloud Cat* to Piper," Gabriel tried again. "Do you read me?"

Still no answer.

"It's getting really rough down here again," Ravi said. "Another storm surge is moving in. Looks worse than the last one."

The Omega sub was bobbing on the surface of the Aqua Gen sea, but Gabriel couldn't see it from his vantage point. The sky below them was swirling with new energy as thunderbolts lit up the darkening clouds. And there was something else: miniature twisters seemed to be forming inside the cloud cover.

"Siena is coming down, I can see her now," Ravi reported.

"Drop the cables, Siena," Anna ordered. "There's no time to reload the sub. We need to get off this planet. Now!"

"We're abandoning our vessel!" Ravi yelled. The Alpha crew could hear the wind and the rain surrounding the Omega team. "Siena's taking us up on cables."

Dash and Gabriel exchanged a look. They needed help, and it was obvious that the Omega team was ditching them. Time to call STEAM. Dash opened a line to the mother ship. "*Cloud Cat* to *Cloud Leopard,* do you read me?" Dash asked. "Come in, *Cloud Leopard.*"

"I'm here. How is the extraction going?" It was Chris, unexpectedly answering the call. "I trust it was smooth and you encountered no one, as planned?"

Gabriel couldn't believe how wrong Chris was. "So, STEAM hasn't briefed you on the events of the day?" he asked, incredulous.

"I'm still in the engine room," Chris said. "I've just completed a twenty-one-hour modification on the slogger. I must say, it was taxing even for me. I had forgotten how temperamental these robots are. My own fault I suppose. I invented them. But you see—"

"Listen, Chris?" Gabriel broke in. "We don't have time for a blow-by-blow right at the moment. It's a little complicated down here."

Chris could hear the stress in Gabriel's voice. "Tell me what you need."

"Were you ever in a really bad storm down here?

We're just above the cloud line, and the formations are like nothing I've ever seen."

"Swirling cones with hollow openings? Lots of them?"

"Yeah, that's exactly right. It's like gnarly twisters as far as the eye can see. And we need to go back down there."

"I have seen this before," Chris said, sprinting toward the navigation deck. "Under no circumstances are you to get any closer to the surface of Aqua Gen until this storm passes. The odds of survival in the *Cloud Cat* are—"

"Nine-hundred-seventy-three to one," STEAM's voice broke in.

"Nine—" Chris started, but Gabriel cut him off.

"We heard."

"Dash, unless there is a very important reason to do this, I highly advise against it," Chris said.

Dash looked at his crew. He couldn't make this decision for them. "Do we go?"

"Of course we do," Carly said without hesitation.

"Why are you even asking?" Gabriel said. "If there's even a chance she's okay, we're going. I was made for flying in this kind of storm. Bring it on."

Dash nodded. They were the Alpha team, and one of their own was in trouble. Nothing would stop them from trying to save her.

The cone-shaped clouds below were swirling angrily like water down a drain. It was a storm like nothing any of them had seen before. But their friend was down there, and that meant everything.

"Let's bring her home."

Dash's order was all Gabriel needed to hear. "Better buckle up, ladies and gentlemen. This is going to be a bumpy ride."

"Wait!" Chris yelled.

Chris never yelled. It was a big deal.

"I'm sorry, Chris," Dash said as he secured himself into the captain's chair. "Piper is down there alone. We have to go."

"I understand," Chris said, his cool monotone returning. "Just wait long enough for me to send some help."

"Help?" Gabriel asked.

"She's a thousand feet from the surface, Dash," Carly said. "And she's got maybe twenty minutes of oxygen left. I'm not sure what it's like down there, but if it's anything like these clouds, we need to hurry."

"Help will arrive in under ten minutes," Chris said. "Please don't go yet."

Carly did some fast calculating work and nodded at Dash.

"Okay, ten minutes," Dash relayed to Chris. "Not a second more."

On the *Cloud Leopard,* Chris turned to STEAM 6000.

"I need ten thousand ZRKs. Pronto."

The waiting was killing the Alpha crew, no one more than Gabriel.

"This storm is only going to get worse. I say we go now."

Dash had been counting the minutes—seven so far—and he was starting to think the same thing. But he trusted Chris, and he knew they could use any help they could get. He was imagining the *Cloud Cat* being spun like it was inside a washing machine, breaking apart as they careened toward Aqua Gen.

"She's connected!" Carly shouted. "Piper is back online."

"Piper, do you read me?" Dash's panicky voice filled the ship, but Piper didn't answer.

"Quiet," Gabriel said. "I hear something."

They all listened as carefully as they could. At first, Dash heard only the distant sound of the storm raging below them in the clouds. But then he heard it too. They all did.

"Is that a dog panting?" Carly asked. "Rocket? That you, boy?"

Rocket barked several times.

"It is Rocket!" Gabriel said. "At least we know the Alpha sub is in one piece."

"Piper, do you read me? Come in, Piper," Dash tried again.

There was no answer.

"Rocket must have activated the communication feature on Piper's wrist tech," Carly said. "All he'd need to do is bump the right icon with his paw."

"Chris, what's the status on this help you're sending us?" Dash asked.

"On the way. Any second now," Chris said. "I'm programming from here."

"Programming what?" Gabriel asked.

"The Alpha sub is only seven hundred feet from the surface," Carly said. "At this rate, it will crest into the storm in about nine minutes."

Ten minutes had officially passed, and Dash was done waiting.

"We're going, Chris. We have to."

"Yes!" Gabriel said, engaging thrusters as he pointed the *Cloud Cat* toward the raging clouds below. He was *so* ready to roll.

"Piper?" Gabriel tried once more. "Hold tight. If you can hear us, we're coming to get you."

The *Cloud Cat* started its descent, slowly edging lower and lower, until Gabriel had them right at the edge of the swirling cloud bank. The wind ripped across the *Cloud Cat,* sending it bucking.

"Are you sure you can do this, Gabriel?" Dash asked.

"Nope. But I'm sure gonna try."

"Formation approaching," Chris said. "You'll know what to do."

"What's he talking about?" Gabriel asked. He had his hands on the manual controls, ready to make a dive into the unknown. There was no way he was letting a computer do this one for him.

"Six hundred feet," Carly said as the *Cloud Cat* was buffeted hard on the right, tipping the vessel sideways.

By the time Gabriel had the ship stabilized again, the help had arrived. Ten thousand ZRKs blew by them on both sides like a swarm of locusts. The noise blotted out the storm, a buzzing, whirling wall of sound as the ZRKs plunged into the clouds. Gabriel thought it was the coolest thing he'd ever seen in his life.

"I love you, Chris!" Gabriel yelled, punching the throttle full tilt and heading into the storm. "Best alien ever!"

"What are they doing?" Carly asked.

As if in answer, the ZRKs spun into a formation that matched one of the large twisters. They were going right for the eye of the storm, creating a giant drill into the inner core of the spiral. Once they were inside, they pushed outward, opening the center to create a safe passage for the *Cloud Cat* to enter.

"Whoa," Dash said. "This is unbelievable."

As the ship entered the middle of the twister, the whole crew went slack-jawed at what they were seeing.

"It's like we're going down the rabbit hole," Carly said, a smile of wonder on her face. "It can't be real."

But it was, and Gabriel was shooting toward the waters of Aqua Gen at top speed. The ZRKs spun in a wide circle all around them, corkscrewing a passage through the eye of the biggest storm any of them had ever been in.

A crack of lightning fired through the center of the ZRKs, blowing dozens of them out of formation. The ship lurched to one side and began spinning.

"Hang on, you guys!" Gabriel shouted. "We're almost through."

The formation continued to dissolve into chaos as the ZRKs fought the toughest part of the tempest. Some of them were holding, but many were firing around the center of the tube.

"Time to really see what this thing can do," Gabriel said calmly. He pressed a series of buttons, and the *Cloud Cat* hit a whole new speed.

The ship blew past all the ZRKs, bumping them out of the way, and shot through the bottom of the clouds into open air.

"Woooooo-hooooooooooo!" Gabriel yelled.

The water was coming up fast, huge waves cresting at fifty feet or more.

"Pull up!" Dash yelled, white-knuckling the armrests.

Gabriel reeled back with all his weight, gripping the throttle with everything he had. The *Cloud Cat* touched down on the water, slid wildly, and gained air again. Dead ahead, a wall of water was rising into a wave big enough to swallow Godzilla whole. Gabriel banked a hard right, hitting the wave with the bottom of the ship and riding. The *Cloud Cat* leveled out, pushed forward by the wave, gaining even more speed.

"We're way off course," Carly said. "She's due north one-point-three miles."

"I see it," Gabriel said, watching the Alpha sub GPS as it blinked on a screen in front of him. He completed a maneuver that required him to drive the ship straight up into the sky, turn and twist hard, and ram the throttle once more.

The ship was pounded by gusts of wind that seemed to come from every direction, but she held as they cut the distance to Piper.

Gabriel looked at the fuming sea and couldn't imagine a tiny submarine riding those waves. It wouldn't last very long.

"Approaching GPS location," Carly said. "She's going to summit this sea any second now."

"I have the ZRKs back in formation," Chris piped in from the *Cloud Leopard*. "We've lost twelve percent of them, but the escape route should hold when you're ready."

Gabriel spotted the swarm of ZRKs on his radar. "I can get us there in no time. Come on, Piper!"

Gabriel struggled to hold the *Cloud Cat* in position above the waves. Sideways rain pummeled the ship, and lightning cracked in white splinters all around them.

"I can't hold too much longer," Gabriel said. "The *Cloud Cat* is going to break up down here if we stay more than another minute or two."

Like a bad omen, a lanky piece of the ship broke off and clattered across the windshield.

"There goes our TV reception," Gabriel clowned.

Dash was laser-focused on the water, watching with the patience of a cat stalking a bird. The clouds were nearly black with rain, sending sheets of water across the *Cloud Cat*. It was hard to see anything but water, water, and more water.

"There!" Carly yelled, pointing slightly to the left of where Dash had been looking.

He shifted his gaze and saw it too. The Alpha sub had surfaced and was bouncing on the waves like a Ping-Pong ball.

"Ready bay doors," Dash said. He released seat locks and began moving toward the back of the ship.

"You can't go out there, Dash!" Carly shouted.

But they all knew there was no other way to bring her back. No mechanical solution was going to do it. Someone had to go out there and get Piper.

Dash careened back and forth inside the *Cloud Cat,* slamming into one wall and then another. When he reached the staging area, he quickly harnessed up and tugged on the cable. He grabbed two more harnesses and slung them over a shoulder. He threw on a helmet and strapped it tight under his chin, setting the communication channel. And then he spoke in a voice that was full of resolve.

"Open bay doors."

At the front of the ship, Gabriel looked at Carly. "Are we really doing this?"

He followed the line of her stare and saw the Alpha sub catch air and slam back into the water.

"Yeah, we're doing this," they both said at the same time.

The bay doors opened, and a swirling rage of wind ravaged the inside of the *Cloud Cat.* Anything that wasn't bolted down was thrust into the air and sucked out into the storm, including Dash Conroy.

"Closing bay doors!" Gabriel said, and with a swooshing sound that deafened the ears, the world of Aqua Gen was sealed out.

Carly controlled the cable and held Dash aloft, just above the water line. It was tricky business, like playing a video game, because the waves rolled up and down at different levels. Carly had to be very precise with her fingers on the screen to keep Dash from slamming into the sea.

"You got this, Carly," Gabriel said.

A bead of sweat rolled down Carly's nose, but she didn't bother wiping it away.

"Moving in," Gabriel said, desperately trying to stay as smooth as possible in the buffeting wind.

"I see the sub!" Dash yelled, and then he realized he wouldn't be able to remove the Energy Glass that served as the sub's windows. "You guys, I'm not going to be able to get her out. The Energy Glass!"

Gabriel quickly called Chris.

"I have another job for your ZRK army. You ready, Chris?"

"Ready to deploy on your order."

Gabriel explained the problem, and in fifteen seconds, a dozen ZRKs raced across the water.

"Come on, Piper," Carly said out loud. She'd lost the rhythm of the sea and dunked Dash below the water line a few feet from the Alpha sub.

When he resurfaced, Dash saw Rocket in the sub, and the golden retriever began to bark excitedly. Then a wave bounced the watercraft up into the air, and it landed again with a crash, righting itself on the water. The dog's head popped up right next to Piper, who wasn't moving.

"Good boy, Rocket!" Dash yelled, though he knew the dog couldn't hear him.

Rocket nuzzled in close to Piper. He really was the best dog in the universe.

Dash saw the ZRKs coming in fast and heard Chris's voice in his helmet. "On your count. ZRKs ready."

Dash had to time it just right. He watched the line of waves rolling toward the sub and waited until just the perfect moment.

"Three, two, one, release ZRKs!"

The ZRKs moved in lightning fast, surrounding the Energy Glass. Tiny arms emerged, and light that looked like welding sparks encircled the top half of the Alpha sub. Dash shielded his eyes, and when he looked again, the ZRKs had removed the Energy Glass. They flew off in formation as Dash dangled precariously on the long line of cable.

"Bring me in fast!" Dash yelled. "There's not much time before the next wave rises up and sinks the sub."

Carly was already moving Dash the few extra feet he needed. A gust of wind suddenly knocked the *Cloud Cat* sideways, and Dash swung on the line like the pendulum on a grandfather clock.

"Lower!" Dash commanded.

"What did he say?" Carly asked. The communication system was failing.

"We've gotta get him lower," Gabriel said.

Carly dropped Dash fast, about five feet from the sub,

submerging him once more and stopping his swinging in the process. When he erupted out of the water, Dash grabbed hold of the Alpha sub. He clung to its slick metal as the storm raged on, climbing up and staring down into the opening.

The sub was already taking on water as Rocket barked.

"Come on, boy, you first," Dash said, holding out one of the two harnesses. But the dog wouldn't budge. He wasn't moving from Piper's side until she was safely out of danger.

152

Dash reached in and unstrapped Piper's shoulder belts. A wave began to rise up behind Dash, ominous and dark.

"Dash, hurry!" Carly said.

Dash finished strapping Piper into a harness and attached her to the cable. He looked up. There would be no time to harness Rocket.

"You ready to go now?" Dash asked.

Rocket barked, and as the shadow of a wave came down over the top of them all, he jumped into Dash's arms. Rocket was a big dog, but Dash hugged him and held on as the *Cloud Cat* ascended into the sky. The very top of the wave washed over Dash, Piper, and Rocket, momentarily submerging them. The Alpha sub turned over, filled with water, and began its long journey to the bottom of the AquaGen sea. When the Alpha team emerged into the pocket of open air between the water below and the swirling, stormy sky above, Dash barely had a hold of Rocket. The dog shivered and laid his head on Dash's shoulder. And then Dash had one of the best moments of his entire life.

Piper woke up.

When the bay doors closed, Gabriel flew into action with more purpose than ever before. He knew he was a great pilot. Even as a kid playing video games, he knew he had skills. But never in his life had he carried such important cargo through such a perilous journey. His bravado vanished. There was no place for that now. One of his friends was in trouble, and he had to get her home safely.

He heard enough of the chatter going on around him to know it was serious, but it was only background noise.

"She was awake when I was out there," Dash said. "She opened her eyes and smiled at me. She coughed up some water."

Dash had strapped her in next to him, scrunching in close on the captain's chair. Her legs were so thin she barely took up any room at all. Carly was rubbing Piper's arms. Dash was holding her hands.

"She's hypothermic," Carly said. "The heating system

must have shut down when she was making the extraction. We need to get her back to the *Cloud Leopard*. STEAM and Chris will know what to do."

Dash looked again at Rocket, who was covered in fur. He'd been able to stand the cold longer than Piper. "You saved her, Rocket. You kept her warm."

The *Cloud Cat* lurched to one side and back again.

"Entering the hive," Gabriel said. "Hold on."

They followed the ZRKs back into the cone of the storm.

Dash, Carly, and Gabriel took one last look at the world of Aqua Gen. They hadn't come away with the element they needed, but the mission didn't feel like a failure somehow.

It was a rocky ride up into the clouds, but they'd done it once before and knowing what to expect made it easier. Before they knew it, the *Cloud Cat* burst into the atmosphere above the clouds. The wind died and the ship quieted to a whisper.

"Clear of the hive," Gabriel said. "Sixteen minutes to rendezvous with *Cloud Leopard*."

"You sound almost like a commander," Carly said.

Gabriel smiled.

Rocket laid his wet head on Piper's legs and stared up into her eyes.

"It's okay, boy. She just needs a little more time," Dash said. But he was no doctor. The doctor was Piper.

He'd trained as her backup, but he didn't really know what was going on or when she would come to. He felt paralyzed. Maybe that look, above the raging sea, was the last time Dash would see her eyes open.

No one spoke for the next few minutes as the *Cloud Cat* moved quietly upward. They exited the atmosphere of Aqua Gen and entered space, the vastness of the stars laid out before them. But none of that mattered. For the Voyagers, the whole universe was wrapped up in their teammate and friend.

Suddenly, Rocket's head popped up, and if a dog had ever smiled, this one did.

"I'm cold."

Dash turned toward Carly, somehow thinking she had said the words. But Carly was staring at Piper. When Dash looked too, Piper was staring right at him.

"We're almost home," Dash said. He couldn't believe it when a tear rolled down his cheek. Piper wiped it away with a half-frozen finger.

"I was afraid I'd lost all of you," she said.

Gabriel put the *Cloud Cat* on autopilot, something he usually couldn't stand doing. He knelt in front of the captain's chair with Rocket and pet his wet fur. "We were afraid we'd lost you too."

The entire Alpha team moved in and touched heads. No one spoke—they didn't have to. They knew how they felt about each other. They were a family.

"I didn't get the element," Piper said. "I'm sorry. I tried."

"Don't think about that," Dash said.

"Anna got it," Piper said. "So at least one of the teams has the element we need."

Piper didn't say anything more about what had happened at the bottom of the Aqua Gen sea. Instead, she leaned forward and gently put her hand on Rocket's head. "Good boy."

A few seconds later, STEAM 6000's voice filled the cabin of the *Cloud Cat.* "Docking in thirty seconds."

Before the ship pulled in, they looked down once more at Aqua Gen. Only a small part of the surface was covered in clouds. The rest was blue and green.

"It looks so peaceful from a distance," Carly said.

"Don't let it fool you," Piper said. "She's got spunk."

They laughed as the bay doors closed.

They weren't back on Earth, and maybe they never would be. But more than ever before, they were home.

Piper was in bed when the call came in. Only an hour had passed, and she was feeling much better, but the crew wasn't going to let her get back to work without some rest. Rocket was all dried off, lying beside her.

"We got a connection with Commander Phillips," Dash said. He carried a tablet with him.

Shawn's face appeared on the monitor. He looked tired.

"Hello, Piper. Dash told me all about your big adventure. I'm glad you're all right."

"Thank you, sir. I didn't get the element. Sorry about that."

Shawn looked uncomfortable for a moment. He paused before saying, "For once, I'm happy there are two ships up there. I'm sure something can be worked out in the end."

"I hope so," Piper said.

"Let me worry about the Pollen Slither. You just get some rest."

Piper nodded and laid her head back against the pillows. Dash took the tablet and walked out of the room, carefully closing the door behind him.

Commander Phillips addressed Dash. "You doing okay, Captain?"

Dash took in a shaky breath. He remembered the ship's log he'd sent out and figured Shawn had listened to it.

"We didn't get the Pollen Slither. And now we're behind schedule. And things could have gone seriously wrong with Piper on her own. And—"

"Piper's safe, so be glad of that," Shawn interrupted. "Your whole team made it back safely thanks to you."

He paused, and Dash readied himself for the next part.

"But not getting the element is a problem," Shawn admitted. "You don't have time to go back and try again.

I know the other ship was able to retrieve a sample, but I'm concerned. I'm not sure we'll be able to negotiate with them easily."

Dash's heart sunk. They had failed their mission. How could he have let this happen? Nervously, he reached for the silver ring Somselia had given him that now hung on a string around his neck.

"What's that you've got?" Shawn asked.

Dash held up the ring. "It was a gift, from the captain of the AquaGens. It's just a ring made out of—" He stopped. It was a ring made out of Pollen Slither! He knew it was a long shot, but could it be possible?

"Sir, I know we need pure, unmanipulated Pollen Slither for the Source," Dash spoke rapidly. "But what if we had a different form of Pollen Slither. Could we make that work?"

Dash held up the ring again, and Shawn caught on. "I doubt it," he replied slowly. Dash's face fell. Shawn sighed. "But maybe it's worth a try. Have Chris do some tests on that ring and see if he can make it work. It's better than nothing."

Dash nodded, hopeful. "Yes, sir."

"All right. Now about the next mission: it's going to be a real challenge. Are you up to the task?"

"I am," Dash said. "We all are."

"You're a day or two behind schedule, so it will be best to jump to Gamma Speed as quickly as you can."

"Yes, sir."

"But before you do, I have something I'd like to share with the crew," said Commander Phillips. "Can you get everyone together?"

Dash, Carly, and Gabriel gathered next to Piper, who lay in her bed. They were all exhausted and defeated. What they really needed was some positive reinforcement—but with Commander Phillips, they knew it could just as easily be bad news as good.

"You've reached the halfway point of your journey," Commander Phillips said. "I can't think of a better time to share some news from home."

Every breath was held, every eye locked on the screen.

The tablet filled with a montage of waves and smiles from people all over the world, cheering them on. There were banners and signs with messages like *Come home soon! We're rooting for you!* A small boy held up a poster board that said *Voyagers rule!* Big crowds of cheering fans swirled into the screen, one group after another, all of them wishing the Voyagers well.

"These are the letters I'm holding for you back home," Commander Phillips said as the screen changed to a room full of mail piled in boxes. "Over five million letters. And that's not including the email—it pours in even faster."

Next came a man with a broad smile and big blue

eyes sitting next to a woman with long blond hair. Her eyes were even bluer and rounder than the man's. Piper gasped and pulled Rocket closer. "It's my mom and dad."

"Hello, Piper," her dad said. "We're very proud of you."

"And we miss you," Piper's mom said. "Earth just isn't the same without you here. Be safe. Don't take any chances you don't have to."

They told her they loved her and then they were gone. Piper reached out for the screen like she wished she could jump inside.

"These are recordings, so I'm afraid you can't speak to them," Commander Phillips said. "Here's another."

Carly's sisters appeared, flanked by her parents. They spoke in Japanese, so none of the other Voyagers could understand what they were saying. Dash thought it sounded like they were encouraging her. Carly said something in Japanese. She nodded and sat down on the edge of the bed as the family vanished. Carly looked reinvigorated.

Gabriel's entire family appeared next. His parents, along with five kids, were all on a big bed and the kids were using it as a bouncing castle. As they leapt from one side to the next, Gabriel's dad laughed and smiled.

"I see where you get your energy," Carly joked.

"What a bunch of knuckleheads," Gabriel said, but he was beaming. It was obvious he loved them all.

"Hey, champ," Gabriel's dad said. "We miss you, buddy."

"And we hear you're doing a very good job out there," Gabriel's mom said. She couldn't fight back the tears and turned away from the camera.

All the kids started cheering and bouncing even higher.

"Your fan club is alive and well," Gabriel's dad said. "And you'll be home before you know it. Hang in there. We're thinking of you always."

Gabriel turned away from the screen as it faded to black. No one could tell for sure, but it looked like he was wiping away a tear.

Last were Dash's mom and sister, staring straight into the screen. His mom took a deep breath and so did Dash. They stared at each other across the universe, barely blinking. A long moment passed, and Dash felt so much relief seeing her, knowing she was waiting for him. The long stare was just what he needed, to simply lay eyes on her.

"I had this all figured out, what I was going to say," Dash's mom said. "But now it's all jumbled up in my head. All I can think about is how far away you are. I look up at the stars every night and try to imagine: *Where's my Dash? What's he doing today?* I know you're strong, stronger than I am. Just hold on a little longer. Before you know it, you'll be turning for home."

She pointed to her eye, then her heart, then Dash. It

was a message they'd sent each other from across many rooms over many years. *I. Love. You.* As Dash did the same, he knew his mom couldn't see him. But it didn't change the fact that she had sent her love and he was sending his all the way through space and time. Home felt closer than ever.

Commander Phillips appeared again.

"We need to get into Gamma Speed in a few minutes," he said. "It will take you farther still from the ones you love and the people who cheer for you every day. The world is depending on you to be strong. It's a lot to ask, I know. But I chose the right crew for the job. You can do it. We're all *expecting* your safe return."

Chris piped in from the bridge. "If it were up to me, there's no other crew I would choose. These truly are the best of the best, sir."

"Agreed," Dash said as he looked around the room at the team who had already gone through so much.

"Until we speak again," Commander Phillips relayed, nodding once and closing the connection.

Dash wasn't quite sure what to do next. He glanced at the floor and folded his arms across his chest.

"I'm not sure how many of you noticed, but I ran the tubes in record time a few days ago," Gabriel said. He looked at the exit and raised an eyebrow. "I think I can better it."

"I think *I* can better it," Carly challenged. She was out the door before Gabriel could cut in front of her, the two of them off to ride the wind.

Dash was about to leave as well, but Piper reached out her hand. "Could you stay for one more minute? There's something I need to talk with you about."

Dash moved in closer and sat down on the edge of the bed. Rocket was asleep, his head on Piper's thin legs.

"I think he's worn out from all the adventure," Dash said quietly.

"STEAM said something to me while you were out of communication on Aqua Gen," Piper began. "He said someone on this ship has a medical condition. It sounded serious. But I'm the ship's doctor and all my testing is up to date. Everyone is fine."

Dash didn't know how to respond. It was a big secret he wasn't supposed to share with anyone, but he and Piper had been through so much together. How could he keep her out of the loop any longer, especially since she was the *Cloud Leopard* medic?

"There is one person I haven't had any access to," Piper conceded. "Chris. He won't let me anywhere near him when it comes to making sure he's operating on all cylinders. Not that I'd know how to diagnose an alien. Maybe his blood is green. Do you think he's okay?"

Dash ran a hand through his hair. "It's not Chris. Chris is fine."

Piper tilted her head, calculating every test and wondering what she'd missed.

Dash took a deep breath.

"It's me," Dash confessed. "I'm the one STEAM was talking about."

Piper sat up straight in bed. "But that's impossible. I've tested you every week for months. Either I'm a lousy doctor or there's nothing wrong with you."

"Yet," Dash said.

Piper's brow cinched tight.

"What's that supposed to mean, *yet*?"

Dash knew it was his call. In the end, so far from central command, he had to reveal information to his crew when he felt it was the right time.

"I'm going to ask you to keep this between us, as the ship's doctor. Can you do that?"

"You're scaring me," Piper said. She put a hand on Rocket and the dog stirred. "Doctor-patient confidentiality extends to the farthest reaches of space. Tell me."

And so Dash told Piper everything. Piper didn't interrupt. She let Dash go through the details of Gamma Speed science and didn't speak until he was done. He told her he was too old for the mission. He told her about the daily injections. He made sure she understood he would be fine, so long as the mission didn't go too long.

"Is that everything?" Piper asked.

"Yeah, that's it," Dash answered. "And I'm sorry I couldn't tell you sooner. Commander Phillips would rather I kept it to myself. I think that was the right call too."

The conversation was on Piper's turf now, and she was suddenly confident and commanding. "For starters, I need to be administering these shots. No one else is more qualified. And I need to speak with Chris about this so I can develop some new tests. I need to be analyzing you daily, not weekly. You need to trust me on this one, Dash."

Dash nodded and thought about his options. "I'll talk with Chris, but let's not go any wider than that. I'm feeling great, no problems. And we're not that far behind schedule. We're going to make it."

Piper nodded, and Dash could tell she was already dreaming up new assessments to track his aging.

She looked right at Dash with those piercing blue eyes of hers. "It was scary on Aqua Gen. There was a moment when I thought I wasn't ever coming back. But you didn't leave me behind. You fought for me. I'm not going to let you die out here either. We're going to make it."

Piper took her tablet and began tapping out notes. She spoke without looking up. "We need you to go immediately into Gamma Speed. There's not a second to waste."

Dash was about to call Chris when STEAM's voice

entered the room through the on-board communication system.

"I have an incoming communication from the *Light Blade*. How would you like to proceed?"

"Send the call ship-wide. Everyone should hear whatever they have to say."

"Communication link established," STEAM said. "Visual and audio."

Dash picked up his tablet and saw Anna's face staring at him.

"Colin and Chris are synced up," Anna said, all business. "We're ready for Gamma Speed whenever you are."

"Piper's doing fine, in case you were wondering," Dash said. He couldn't help himself. How could Anna be so cold to not even ask?

"I know that already. Chris relayed earlier. I'm glad she's feeling better. You guys need a doctor on that ship with all the chaos you're getting yourselves into."

"No thanks to you, Anna," Dash shot back.

Anna held up a glass sphere. It was about the size of a baby bottle and was full of glowing blue-and-green liquid. She tipped it to one side, and the liquid moved like lava inside a lava lamp.

"Pollen Slither," Dash said. He wished he could reach out and take it from her.

"You should see it close up," Anna taunted. "The monitors don't do it justice. It glows like neon. Incredible."

"I get it, Anna. You have the element and we don't. Is there a point to this call?"

Anna looked straight into the screen. "This is our insurance policy, Dash. You lose us out here in space and we're both toast. Now we're linked. You can't leave us behind."

"We would never have left you behind, you know that."

"So you say. But you're not really in charge, are you, Dash Conroy? You answer to Shawn Phillips, and last time I checked, he was a lying, incompetent jerk. I prefer being in control."

"We need each other more than ever," Dash said. "We're on the same team."

"No, we're not. That's your problem, Dash. You're weak. I'm not on your team. And you better watch your back. Omega is on the rise."

"Are we through here?" Dash asked.

"I don't know, are we?"

Dash cut the communication. He wanted to throw the tablet against the wall, and he might have if Piper wasn't right there with him. He couldn't make her feel responsible for missing their chance to get the element.

"Ready for Gamma Speed?" Gabriel asked.

"Ready," Piper said.

Gabriel opened a line to the main deck. "Let's get out of here. On my count."

"Secured," Chris said from somewhere in the ship. It was their code word for being strapped in, ready for the g-forces that starting into Gamma Speed produced.

"Secured," Carly said.

Dash secured Piper and Rocket to the bed with three separate straps. He settled into a chair mounted against the wall and locked in.

"Secured," Piper said.

Gabriel took a deep breath and gave the order.

"Gamma Speed in three, two, one."

Piper closed her eyes and imagined the watery world of Aqua Gen getting smaller and smaller until it was gone from view forever.

The *Light Blade* took chase, following the heat signature of massive speed as they raced across the universe tailing the *Cloud Leopard*. They would travel for many days at this speed, until they reached their next destination and the fourth of six elements.

Within an hour of entering Gamma Speed, Anna had her crew training for the next round of challenges. It would be perilous and hard fought, but she fully expected to gain the upper hand once more when the time came. Her team would be ready. She kept the Pollen Slither at her side on the main deck. Eventually she would deposit it into the vault, but for now, she liked to look at it.

Farther back in the ship, the engine room was humming with ZRKs as Colin worked to keep the ship running smoothly. He was grumbling as usual, angry that the Omega team had managed to extract yet another element without very much help from him. But he was also sick and tired of working on all the *Light Blade*'s problems. Gamma Speed was always the most dangerous time for the *Light Blade*. He was on high alert, sending out swarms of ZRKs to monitor various parts of the massive Gamma Speed engine system. Colin had been so absorbed in keeping the shaky ship running and plotting how to take over command, he hadn't taken the time to think of anything else. But even if he had, there's no telling if he would have known where the real danger lay on his ship.

Farther back still, in a secure vault off to the side of the engine room, two of the elements they'd already retrieved were stored.

There in the vault, behind the closed metal door, something rattled.

The slogger they'd used to retrieve Magnus 7 from Meta Prime was shaking. It rocked back and forth. It walked a circle. Steam poured from its head. The metal body began to expand like a balloon, its surface burning red.

The slogger made something like the sound of a burp and seemed to settle down. The metal retracted and returned to its normal color.

The slogger coughed twice.

How long could it hold Magnus 7 before breaking down entirely, releasing a substance that would quickly destroy the *Light Blade*?

Only time would tell.

Find the Source. Save the World.

Follow the Voyagers to the next planet!

SIGN ON. JOIN THE CREW. SAVE THE WORLD!

VOYAGERS

4

INFINITY RIDERS

KEKLA MAGOON

The *Cloud Cat* skimmed the surface of Infinity. Gabriel, Carly, and Chris looked out the windows and studied the rocky terrain in awe.

"No wonder nothing survives on the surface," Carly said. "It's completely barren." There wasn't so much as a blade of grass or a river in sight. The smooth rock shone gray, awash in predawn light. The view created a somber mood in the landing craft.

In the distance, light glinted off the corner of something metal looming up on the horizon.

"Set it down over there," Chris said. "That's the Jackal compound."

Gabriel brought the *Cloud Cat* to a smooth stop on the flattest stretch of rock he could find.

"This may be our last chance to communicate with the *Cloud Leopard*," Chris informed them. "Once we're underground, the rock will most likely block our signal."

"At least they'll see we've landed safely," Carly said. "We'll get in touch later if we can."

They exited the landing craft one by one, and slowly made their way toward the compound's entrance. Very slowly. It felt like their feet were weighted down.

"Is it me, or is it harder to move than it should be?" Gabriel asked. He felt kind of like he was walking through water.

"Oh, right. This is the gravity issue I mentioned," Chris said. "The planet's core is very dense. It's the gravity."

"Seriously," Carly said. "It's kind of a workout."

It wasn't too bad once they got used to it. By the time they reached the tall metal doors, they barely noticed the bit of extra energy it took to walk.

Chris knocked on the door. The thick metal sheet thumped and rattled as he pounded.

"I'm sure they've seen us by now," he commented, pointing up at a massive fish-eye lens mounted on the upper edge of the door frame.

They waited.

And waited.

Nothing happened.

Carly glanced around, slightly nervous. Even though there was no specific threat on the surface of Infinity, she wanted to remain alert. On their last mission, the danger started the moment they set down on a planet.

Chris pounded on the door again.

Nothing.

"Very strange," he said.

Gabriel shrugged. "We can greet the Jackals later. How do we get to the caves?"

"There are many entrances, but the most direct route is through their outpost," Chris answered. "They've built access tunnels. And mapped the interior."

Gabriel reached for the door handle. He twisted the knob, and the door swung open inward, revealing a dark foyer.

"We can't enter without permission," Chris protested. "That definitely goes against Jackal hospitality protocol."

"We need those maps," Gabriel insisted. "We're on a schedule here."

"We don't have a choice," Carly agreed. She followed Gabriel into the dim space.

As they stepped inside, a string of bulbous orange lights illuminated the space. They were like the strings of bulbs people put on their roofs around the holidays, only much bigger. The size of gallon milk jugs.

The foyer narrowed to a corridor that wound slightly downhill. The lights along each row came on one by one, until disappearing around the bend at the bottom of the hill.

Chris took the lead, apparently coming around to agree that they had to proceed.

The corridor ended in a large living room. The space was full of institutional furniture, like you might find in a dentist's waiting room. Rows of slightly cushioned chairs with upholstery that looked like leather, separated by low coffee tables. More of the bulbous orange lamps stuck out of the tables like crystal balls or neon pumpkins. The whole place had a warm, fiery glow.

Gabriel touched the back of one of the chairs. It was slick, gray-green, and vaguely familiar. "Is it me, or does that look like . . . ?"

Chris nodded. "Sawtooth skin. Good for all-weather clothing and upholstery. Very durable."

Carly and Gabriel exchanged a glance. Skinning Saws didn't sound like anyone's idea of fun.

Several dark corridors snaked away from the central waiting room. As soon as Carly walked toward the mouth of one hall, it lit up. Like the entryway, the corridor was lined with strings of colored lights on both sides. Instead of being all orange, it was only orange on the left. The string of lights on the right hand side was all green.

Gabriel walked toward a different hallway, and that one lit up orange and blue. It turned out that the lights in each hallway had orange, plus a different color. Green. Blue. White. Brown. Red.

"It's for navigation," Chris explained. "The left-hand lights stand for the room you are coming from. The right-hand lights tell you which room you're going to."

"That's smart."

"Jackals are an advanced race," Chris said. "The team on Infinity is primarily explorers and research scientists. Everything is systematized." He glanced around. "If I recall correctly, green leads to the research division. They must be down there working."

"Maybe that's why they didn't hear us knock," Carly suggested.

They followed the green lights. The corridor led to a cluster of glass-walled laboratories.

Dozens of labs.

None were occupied.

In fact, none looked like they had been occupied for a very long time.

The first lab they entered contained a lot of complicated-looking machinery. There were shelves of test tubes, graduated cylinders, and what looked like neon Tupperware. Lights glowed on some of the machines, but none emitted any sound. Not even the barest hum of a running refrigerator.

Gabriel ran his finger over the countertop and picked up a layer of dust. He wiped it quickly on his pants, and shivered slightly. This eerie outpost, with its abandoned labs, totally skeeved him out.

"They've gone," Chris said, sounding disappointed. "When they didn't answer the door, I knew something wasn't right."

"They left all their stuff, it looks like," Gabriel said.

Carly added, "Maybe we'll still find something we can use."

The next lab appeared to be devoted to the study of Stingers. One wall had a grid of small and medium-sized animal cages, like you might find full of mice or birds in a biology lab back on Earth. They were empty.

The wall held a series of anatomical pictures of Stingers: front view, side views, top view, belly view. A close-up on the wicked barbed tail. Framed beside it was a real live skeleton under glass. And beside that, a detailed artist's rendering of the Stinger's internal organs.

Gabriel took a close look at the skeleton. "So this is what we're up against." He grinned. "Doesn't look so terrible."

"Famous last words," Carly muttered.

Carly examined a rack of what appeared to be surgical tools—knives and scalpels, scissors and forceps, mallets and straight pins, tweezers and clamps of all shapes and sizes. "Yikes," she said. "You could do a lot of damage with this arsenal."

Gabriel noticed a small jar of what looked like BBs resting on the countertop. "Hey, look!" he said. "Aren't these the spores we need?"

Chris glanced at the jar. "Yeah, looks like it," he said. "But that is not nearly enough. We need a thousand, remember?"

The jar contained maybe twenty. Gabriel shook it and the spores rattled like a maraca. "That's music to my ears," he said. "Twenty down, only nine thousand, nine hundred, and eighty to go!"

Carly rolled her eyes. "Woo-hoo. We really put a dent in the spore count just now." She laughed, raising her fists in mock-celebration. "But seriously," she added, "maybe we should poke around and look for some more." She started opening cabinets. It made sense to stay positive, but she knew there was no chance they could avoid facing down the live Stingers.

"I doubt these will be fresh enough," Chris warned. "The toxin's potency will have faded over time."

"Better safe than sorry." Jar in hand, Gabriel swung his backpack off and began to unzip it.

"No," Chris said sharply. "We cannot take that without permission."

Gabriel popped the jar into his backpack anyway. "The place is deserted. What's the big deal?"

A slight mechanical sound whirred from somewhere above and behind them.

Carly spun around.

The fish-eye camera mounted high in one corner traced a slow arc within its frame. Carly looked at it for a moment, wondering if someone was looking back at her.

"This place gives me the creeps," Gabriel said. He led the way back into the hall. "Let's get on with it. How do we find these Sawtooth tunnels?"

"Listen," Carly said. A soft whinnying sound carried through the hallways from someplace out of sight. "Do you hear that?"

Gabriel cocked his head and listened. "Yeah, what is it?"

"Sounds like Weavers, maybe," Carly mused.

"It is bad enough that we are in their space without proper admittance," Chris said. His usually monotone voice betrayed a hint of nervousness. "We cannot take too many liberties."

"We have a job to do," Gabriel said. "And no one's here."

With Carly leading the way, they followed the sound. This corridor was lined with green and black lights. Before long, they found themselves at the edge of a deep, high-ceilinged cavern. The entrance to the large open space was protected by a narrow gate of two horizontal bars.

"A quick look won't hurt anything," Chris conceded.

"Since we're already this far inside. But we cannot borrow them without permission." Chris unclasped the gate latch at one side and swung it open.

Carly and Gabriel stepped past him into the Weaver enclosure. The black animals roamed free in their allotted space. Two strolled around the stony pasture, while the other four dipped and swirled in the air, stretching their wings.

"Whoa," Gabriel blurted out. "They really are like horses with wings. Crazy."

The Weavers looked quite real to him, like a thing that could have been found back on Earth, unlike so many of the beings they'd encountered. And yet, they were so clearly "other."

They smelled musky and dark—if a thing could smell dark—and they radiated calmness and grace. One of the Weavers cantered straight toward Carly. It pressed its damp muzzle against her shoulder, sniffing curiously. She reached up and stroked its silken black mane. The strands felt liquid smooth, like passing her hand through a flowing stream of water.

"Hey, you," she whispered. "How are you? Nice to meet you."

The Weaver whinnied, sounding so much like an Earth horse that Carly grew homesick. She reached up and hugged the creature's sinewy neck, and the Weaver stood still and allowed it. This is the one she would ride, Carly decided then and there.

Gabriel looked around the edges of the pen. A row of six saddles hung on one wall. Helmets, reins, bits, crops, and other riding gear rested on a set of shelves. Beside that hung a rack of wicked-looking swords.

"Yikes," Gabriel said, upon seeing those long swords. These were definitely not dulled and blunted for sparring. They were the real deal. Each saddle had two fat sword scabbards, one on each side. "Maybe the Jackals sword-fight two-handed. That's nuts."

He backed away from the arsenal slowly. He headed over toward Carly and the Weavers.

"We're going to have to borrow them, permission or not," Carly commented. "Unless there's something you're not telling us about the Jackals, in which case, now would be a good time to clue us in, Chris," she added, turning around.

But Chris was nowhere to be seen.

Far on the other side of Infinity, a second small landing craft skimmed the rocky surface.

"Set down over there," Siena determined. She pointed toward a craggy mountain range jutting up against the sky in the distance. She consulted the hand-drawn sketch of the planet's surface that Colin had given them.

"At the base of those hills, right?" Ravi confirmed.

"Right."

"Is there going to be a door or something?" Niko wondered.

"Probably just a hole in the ground," Ravi said. "I'll try not to set the ship down right in it."

"Yeah, let's avoid getting stuck in a pothole," Siena said.

Silence returned to the *Clipper* landing craft. Pre-mission tension. Everyone had their game face on.

There were plenty of other entrances to the caves that didn't require going through the Jackal compound. Colin's map led to one of them.

From there, they'd have to record their progress through the tunnels carefully so they could find their way back out. Maps were useless underground, Colin had insisted, since the tunnels changed so often.

The Omega crew didn't need any help from the Jackals. They could do it all on their own.

It was better this way.

They'd get in and out, no problem, Colin had assured them. Quick and clean and, hopefully, unnoticed.

"Where did Chris go?" Carly asked. The Weaver cavern seemed bigger and stranger all of a sudden.

Gabriel shrugged. "We'd better find him."

They wandered up the hallway, back in the direction they had come. The empty labs seemed even eerier now, if possible. Other hallways spun off in many directions. Chris could have gone anywhere.

"He can't have just vanished," Gabriel said.

"Or so you think," Carly said, trying to make her voice sound mysterious. It wasn't hard in these surroundings. "Maybe he's been concealing alien teleporting technology from us all this time."

"Ha," Gabriel said. "You think he's going to reappear,

in a tuxedo or something?" He laughed and made jazz hands, shaking his palms out to the sides. "Surprise!"

Carly laughed too. It felt like they needed to fill the silence. The quiet in the labs was too eerie otherwise.

It was extra odd being just the two of them. *Gabriel Parker and Carly Diamond, alone in the vastness of Infinity* . . . The words echoed in her head like a movie-trailer voice-over.

Carly took the opportunity to contact the *Cloud Leopard*. She raised her MTB and tried to radio Dash and Piper.

No luck. The connection failed to produce even static.

Chris had been right—the rock blocked all radio signals to the surface. Plus, the part of the Jackal outpost that was on the surface must have been relatively small. They were definitely deep underground now. The walls here appeared to have been carved straight out of the stone.

"Hey, look at this," Carly exclaimed. She entered one of the labs they hadn't explored yet. It was mostly empty, except for a battered-looking metal safe the size of a mini refrigerator.

The small safe looked like it had been dropped from a great height. It was all crinkled and crushed, like an empty juice box. The smashed metal door had rings for a padlock, but there wasn't one. It didn't appear to be locked—just so damaged that it had become impossible to open.

Gabriel tugged on the door. It didn't budge.

Carly examined the safe from all sides. "There's writing over here." She tapped the MTB on her wrist and brought up their translation program. The crew had a special translator device, but as a safety precaution, Chris had downloaded the program to their MTBs too.

"It translates to 'tunnel navigation system,'" she reported. "Approximately."

Gabriel grinned, excited. "Wait . . . it says 'approximately'?" he asked. "Why would you want to navigate approximately?"

"I think it means it's an approximate translation."

"Oh. That's even weirder." Gabriel took off his backpack and rummaged inside it for a minute. He pulled out a small black pouch.

Carly knocked on the safe's metal walls, as if hoping someone might open it from the inside. "We have to open it," she insisted. "Maybe we can pry the door loose with a screwdriver?"

"Yeah, I have one right in here—" Gabriel unzipped the black pouch."Yahh!" he cried, jumping back in surprise. His padded Simu Suit loomed over him like a ghost.

Carly laughed at his stunned expression. "Why'd you even bring that?"

"I didn't mean to," Gabriel said. "I thought it was my tool pouch. Shoot. I must have picked up the wrong one when I was packing." They were both small black zippered pouches. He could easily see how he'd made the mistake.

"Oh," Carly said. "So we don't actually have your tool pouch on planet?"

Gabriel rummaged in his bag. "I guess not. Sorry."

"It's not a big deal," Carly said. "This place is pretty well stocked. We can probably find any tools we need around here." She scanned the shelves while Gabriel set about refolding the Simu Suit. He squished the foam flatter and flatter and zipped it back into place. He returned the pouch to his backpack, still feeling kind of embarrassed over the confusion.

Carly pulled a scraper from the bottom of a shelf. It had a flat metal head about two inches wide and a thicker blue plastic handle. "Here—why don't we try this set?"

"That works." Gabriel helped Carly position the lip of the scraper in the space along the edge of the safe door. He pushed all of his weight against it.

The door inched open.

The contents of the safe were . . . utterly disappointing.

"It's paint." Carly said. Several stacks of fist-sized canisters. Except they were all the same pale yellow color. Barely yellow, more like a saltine cracker. Each can had a pair of hooks looping off the rim, like quotation marks. Or fangs. A stack of clean brushes accompanied them.

"Well, that was anticlimactic," Gabriel added dryly.

"I guess they've repurposed this safe." Carly poked at the lid of the paint can. "And it's not even a good color."

Gabriel rolled his eyes jokingly. "Haven't you heard? Neon pale is the new black."

"Like I'm ever going to trust your fashion sense," Carly quipped.

He grabbed three cans and started juggling them, only to watch them crash onto the floor and flop in all directions. "Whoa, that is some heavy paint," he said.

"Extra gravity, remember?" Carly reminded him.

"Right." Gabriel bent down and picked a can up by the fangs. He twirled it around his finger. It was heavier than swinging a ceramic mug.

"Let's go," Carly said. "We have to find Chris." She went into the hall. A minute later, Gabriel joined her. He was still messing around in his bag.

"Careful," Carly warned. "You got any other surprises in there?"

Gabriel grinned. "I just might."

They walked past additional labs. Gabriel looked in the door of each, in case anything caught his eye. He felt torn between the creepy fun of exploring the labs, and the need to find Chris and get on with the mission. There might be other useful things to find, but they had a job to do here too.

The corridor dead-ended in a T. The new hallway

was wider than the others had been. There was a row of red bulbs mounted high on the far wall, but that was it. Several appeared shattered.

"Which way now?" Carly asked.

"I guess they stopped putting in lighting at some point," Gabriel said. He flicked on his flashlight and pointed it both ways down the dark hall. Then he shrugged. "This way."

They turned left and made their way down the corridor. The sound of their footsteps became echoey. Beside them, the row of red lights blinked three times, then went out.

"Huh," Gabriel said. "Does this feel right to you?"

"Maybe they're on a timer." Carly pulled out her flashlight too. The dual beams made it somewhat easier to see the path in front of them.

"Oh, look!" Carly said. She hurried through the swath of light toward the thing that had caught her eye. "A flower. Isn't it pretty?"

She bent to examine it. It was hard to tell in the darkness what color it was. Lavender, she thought, or something close. It had a broad flat face, sort of like a daisy, but with thick, round petals that felt full, like aloe leaves. It grew from a flexible, four-stranded stem that curved out of a moss-lined crack in the wall.

When Carly reached down and touched the stem, she wasn't intending to pluck the flower. The stem strands severed seemingly of their own accord. They coiled around her index finger and thumb, gripping like a baby's fist.

"Cool," Gabriel said.

"Why is it growing indoors?" Carly wondered.

"Um, it's not . . . ," Gabriel said, coming up closer behind her. He swept the flashlight over the wall she was crouched near. It wasn't smooth, as if cut by man-made tools. It was made of jagged stone.

The realization dawned slowly. "We're not in the Jackal building anymore," Carly said. This tunnel was more than three times as tall as they were—at least fifteen feet high—and just about that wide. Like a circle. A circle chewed out by giant stone-cutting teeth.

"These are the Sawtooth caves," Gabriel said. He shone the flashlight back the way they had come. All jagged stone, as far as they could see.

"When did it change?" Carly said. "Why didn't we notice?" As she spoke, the flower tendrils coiled snugly, tucking deeper into the spaces between her fingers.

"I don't know. The difference must be subtle at first," Gabriel said. "We were focused on finding Chris."

"Let's get back. We should find him before we go farther," Carly said.

Gabriel agreed. "We need the maps."

"And the Weavers."

They started walking back the way they came. The hallway seemed much longer and darker now.

Carly was the first to hear the scraping sound. "Did you hear that?"

"It's nothing," Gabriel said. "Let's just get back to the Jackal compound."

The scraping sound grew louder. Or . . . closer.

It was a shushing of leathery skin on stone. "Something's coming," Carly said.

Whatever Gabriel was going to say in response was drowned out by the grind of stone-cutting jaws. A massive Sawtooth Land Eel slid around the corner in front of them, gnashing and slathering.

Patrick Carman was obsessed with the idea of traveling into space when he was a kid. He would have loved being a Voyager! Exploring planets, meeting aliens, and saving the world—does it get any better than that? He is also the author of *The Black Circle* (a 39 Clues book), the Skeleton Creek series, the Trackers series, *3:15*, and the Dark Eden series. When Patrick isn't lost on distant planets, he spends his free time supporting literacy campaigns and community organizations, fly-fishing, playing basketball, golfing badly, doing crosswords, watching movies, dabbling in video games, reading (lots), and (more than anything else) spending time with his wife and two daughters.

Visit him online at patrickcarman.com.

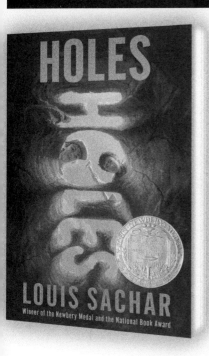

SOME
SECRETS
ARE TOO BIG TO
KEEP
HIDDEN.

Stanley is unjustly sent to a boys' detention center, Camp Green Lake, where the boys build character by spending all day, every day, digging holes exactly five feet wide and five feet deep.

It doesn't take long for Stanley to realize there's more than character improvement going on at Camp Green Lake. The boys are digging holes because the warden is looking for something. But what could be buried under a dried-up lake?

AN EXPERIMENT IN POSSIBILITY.

Eleven-year-old Ellie has never liked change. She misses fifth grade, her old best friend, and even her dearly departed goldfish. Then one day a strange boy shows up. He's bossy and cranky, and he sort of looks like Ellie's grandfather, a scientist who's obsessed with immortality. Could this mysterious boy really be Grandpa Melvin? Has he finally found the secret to eternal youth?

"Discover the coolest library in the world."

—JAMES PATTERSON,
#1 *New York Times* bestselling author of *I Funny*

Kyle Keeley is the class clown and a huge fan of all games. Luigi Lemoncello is the best gamemaker in the world and Kyle's hero . . . and he just so happens to be the genius behind the construction of the new town library.

Join Kyle and Mr. Lemoncello in these puzzle-packed adventures!

NEXT DESTINATION:
INFINITY

The fourth element is hidden somewhere in the maze beneath Infinity's surface. Flying horses carry the fearless Alpha team through the tunnels, dodging deadly Stingers and bone-crushing Saws. But the Omega team is hatching a secret plan—an ambush no one sees coming. . . .

MISSION BRIEFING

ATTENTION: AUTHORIZED PERSONNEL ONLY

All team members must report to headquarters immediately. We have a major situation on our hands—Situation Omega. Your participation is critical to the success of our mission.

- CRACK the book codes
- GO ON Top-Secret Missions
- BUILD your own ZRK Commander
- UNLOCK new ZRKs
- LISTEN TO ship's logs from the crew
- EXPLORE Aqua Gen and its inhabitants

LOG ON NOW AND START YOUR JOURNEY!